DARING TO
LOVE AGAIN

DARING TO LOVE AGAIN

•

Mary Anne Taylor

AVALON BOOKS
NEW YORK

PRINTED IN THE UNITED STATES OF AMERICA
ON ACID-FREE PAPER
BY HADDON CRAFTSMEN, BLOOMSBURG, PENNSYLVANIA

To Jack, my husband and best friend. Thank you for your unflagging inspiration, love, and encouragement. And for keeping my computer running.

To my writing friends: Phyllis, Victoria, Pam and Elaine. Your generosity of spirit always amazes me. Thank you for your enthusiasm, advice, and support.

To my mom and dad, Mary and Edward, who taught me the value of hard work and perseverance.

To Gerry and Kathleen, who inspire me to look for the challenges in life that keep it forever new and exciting.

Chapter One

"Have you seen a gray kitty?" The childish voice startled Jessica. She hadn't heard anyone approach as she struggled to get the last of the moving boxes out of the back seat of her car. She turned to see a small blond girl with worried blue eyes; the dappled sunlight on her cheeks glistened on half-dried tears.

"No I haven't, honey. Have you lost your kitten?" The little girl nodded solemnly. Jessica guessed that she must be about four or five years old. She wore the tiniest pair of blue jeans that Jessica had ever seen and a multi-colored knit top.

"I left the back door open, and he got out. He's only seven weeks old. I'm afraid he'll get lost." The tiny fist of one of her hands pulled on the fingers of the other and she seemed on the verge of tears again.

1

"I'll keep an eye out for him," Jessica assured her, crouching to the child's level. "What's your kitten's name?"

"His name is Smokey." She paused, looking at Jessica thoughtfully for a moment. "Are you our new neighbor?"

"Yes, I'm Jessica Roberts." She extended her hand to the child, who placed her hand in Jessie's. Such a little hand. It evoked a familiar ache.

"I'm Becky," the child replied. "I live next door." Looking in the direction the tiny finger pointed, Jessica observed the lovely Tudor-style home on the other side of her four-foot hedge. She had often admired it while negotiating for and moving into her own home.

Hers was a very small and a very old house on a tiny lot in this affluent suburb. It was all Jessie could afford in this area, but she loved the big old trees and the proximity of the hills here in Woodsborough.

As the child spoke, Jessie became aware of the sound of a car passing slowly. They both looked up to see a gray sedan turn into the driveway of the Tudor style home.

"Oh, my daddy's home!" Becky exclaimed. "Maybe he'll help me find Smokey." She started to run off, but then stopped and scurried back to where Jessica stood. "It was very nice to meet you, bye!" She turned and ran off again, crouching through a low opening in the hedge.

"It was nice meeting you too," Jessica called to the

retreating figure. She watched as Becky ran towards the man who had begun to climb out of the car. The child chattered animatedly as he pulled a briefcase and another parcel from the vehicle.

When he straightened to look at Becky, Jessica couldn't restrain a short intake of breath. The man appeared to be extremely good-looking from this distance. And when he tucked the parcel under the arm that carried the briefcase and then took Becky's small hand in his as they walked towards the house, Jessica repressed a rising feeling of pain and hopelessness. You're here to forget all of that, Jessica, she told herself and to get on with a different kind of life.

Shifting her attention back to the recalcitrant box, Jessica finally yanked it free of its encumbered position in the car. This was the last one. Now she had another several hours of unpacking ahead of her.

Setting the box down in the foyer, she turned to look wistfully outside before closing the door. It was such a beautiful day, she thought, looking at the big old scrub oak trees in her front yard and lifting her head to the warm breeze which filtered through their branches; she wished she had time for a leisurely walk.

But she turned inside with a reluctant sigh, and as she did so, the telephone rang. She walked the short distance to the living room to answer it.

"Hi, honey!" her father's cheerful voice sounded from the other end of the line. "How's the unpacking going"?

"Fine, Dad. Slowly, but surely." Jessica could hear the concern behind her father's cheerfulness. She knew that her parents worried about her being on her own for the first time since Jim's death. Perhaps she was truly on her own for the first time in her life. Just days ago, she had moved more than a hundred miles away from them, to this suburb south of San Francisco, to finish her education.

The first few weeks of the school quarter—before her house had been ready for habitation—she'd driven in from Colesville three days a week, and that had been strenuous. She was happy to have a place of her own closer to campus now.

"We've been thinking about you, all alone out there. Are you okay, honey?"

"I'm doing fine, Dad. Really." Her parents lived in the small rural community near the Sierra foothills where Jessie had grown up. To them, this rapidly developing high-tech area to which she'd moved was the proverbial big city. Of course, she and Jim had lived here together, but in her parents's minds, he'd been taking care of their little girl then. Jessie was an only child, the only child her parents were able to have, and they worried about her.

After reassuring her father that everything was going well and promising to call soon, she said good-bye.

Then Jessica turned to confront the multitude of boxes that still lined one wall of her living room. She spent the next three hours applying herself to the task of unpacking as many as possible.

After a supper of cold tuna salad, Jessica curled up with the evening newspaper on her living room couch. It was an unseasonably warm spring evening, and the living room window was open. A slight breeze drifted in, causing Jessica to look up.

The room faced a small backyard with its concrete patio, meticulously manicured lawn, and small patch of flower garden, all visible through the delightful row of French doors which had been the final inducement in causing Jessie to fall in love with this place. She sighed with contentment. This lovely little house was her home now. The elderly woman from whom she'd bought it had obviously loved and cared for it.

Jessica had considered renting an apartment here initially, but homes were appreciating so rapidly in this area that she'd concluded buying a house would be a good investment. And now, she was so glad that she did.

Smiling, Jessica returned to her paper, but soon the fatigue of the day overcame her attempts to read, and she began to doze.

Suddenly a noise startled her back to wakefulness. It seemed to have come from the backyard, but darkness had fallen, and she could see nothing past the windows.

Someone was back there!

Her heart pounded. Still foggy from sleep, her confused mind struggled to think. It sounded as though something had fallen or been dropped. Unable to move, she sat listening intently.

"Meow." The barely audible plaint wafted to her ear.

In relief, Jessica expelled the breath she'd been holding. She walked to the French doors and opened one of them. Again she heard the soft cry: "Meow." She switched on the patio light.

Just a few feet away, a little gray kitten stood looking up at her, its eyes shining in the glare of the light. And nearby was the fallen broom she had left back there this afternoon. The kitten had probably knocked it over.

Opening the door wider, she coaxed the small kitten to herself. What had the little girl said its name was? Yes, Smokey. "Come here, Smokey, here, kitty," she called.

Hesitantly the kitten came toward her. It was probably hungry if it had been out since the middle of the afternoon. Slowly, cautiously, she reached for it, her hands closing over the soft ball of gray fur. "Well, little Smokey, where have you been hiding?" she murmured as she brought him inside and closed the door. The kitten struggled to free itself, and Jessica let it jump to the floor.

"We'd better let Becky know you're here. She's been worried about you." A glance at the clock told her that it was only 8 o'clock, not too late to return him tonight. She put on her jacket and picked up the kitten.

Lights glowed warmly from the windows of the Tudor-style house as Jessica walked up the driveway. She rang the bell. When the door opened, she found herself looking up at the man she'd seen get out of the car this afternoon. He was tall, dark-haired, and very attractive.

"Hello, I'm . . ." she started to introduce herself.

But the man, looking down into her arms and seeing the kitten, broke into a smile. "Smokey!"

He turned to call into the house. "Becky, look here! Someone's brought Smokey back."

Becky came rushing into the foyer, followed by a sandy-haired boy, a few years older than herself. Both children's faces dissolved into smiles when they saw the kitten. Scooping him from Jessie's arms, Becky cuddled him and cooed, "Smokey, why did you run away, you naughty kitty?" She looked up at Jessica. "Where did you find him?"

"He wandered into my backyard," Jessica explained. Then turning to the man who had answered the door, she extended her hand. "Hello, I'm Jessica Roberts. I just moved in next door." The gentleness with which he took her hand startled her. She found herself looking into smiling hazel eyes.

"Yes, I'd heard the Brower house had a new owner. Welcome to the neighborhood."

"Thank you. I think I'm going to like it here."

"I'm David Bennington. And thank you for bringing Smokey home." The smiling softness of his eyes and the way they looked into her own when he spoke made Jessica feel strangely flustered.

"I . . . I met Becky this afternoon when she was looking for her kitten." Then realizing that her hand was still in his, she retrieved it and shoved it into her jacket pocket.

"Please come in," he said, stepping aside to allow Jessica to enter and then closing the door behind her. "Becky's been worried. I'm sure she'll sleep much better now that Smokey's home."

"Want to see Smokey's bed and all his toys?" Becky piped in. "They're out in the kitchen." She started for the back of the house.

"Well . . ." Jessica glanced uncertainly at the child's father.

He turned an indulgent smile from Becky, then murmured just loud enough for Jessica to hear, "Please indulge her. She and Agatha have been back and forth between here and the pet store all week, picking out just the right toys." He had an air of ease and self-assurance about him. She nodded and followed Becky into the kitchen.

David Bennington watched her go, his eyes taking in her trim, jean-clad form. When she'd introduced herself, those big brown eyes, looking up into his own, had held him transfixed for a moment. The softness of her hand made him reluctant to let go.

When they arrived in the kitchen, he watched as she appeared to show a genuine interest in Smokey's possessions. The bright kitchen light gleamed on her dark brown, nearly shoulder-length hair, which fell forward across her cheeks as she stooped to examine several items.

Becky excitedly showed her the wicker pet bed with its floral-covered cushion and an array of both purchased and homemade toys. Jessica found herself only half listening, preoccupied instead by the child's happy enthusiasm.

She and Jim had wanted children. They'd both been to several doctors. She had, in fact, been pregnant twice but had suffered miscarriages both times. For the last two years of their marriage, they'd tried to accept the inevitable, but the ache and longing for a child of her own never left her.

Jessica struggled to bring her attention back to Smokey's possessions and expressed her admiration for them. Then, refusing a cup of coffee or tea and pleading the fatigue of a long day of unpacking, she turned to leave.

David and the children—she'd learned the boy's name was Tad—insisted on walking her to the end of their driveway and watching until she was inside her own home. She waved to them as she opened her door and stepped inside.

David Bennington continued to stare at the door long after it had closed behind Jessica.

"Come on, Dad. Aren't you coming back into the house?"

"Yeah, Tad. I'm coming." He took a slow step or two, but continued looking in the direction of Jessica's house.

"How come you keep looking over there? She got in the house okay."

David gave a wistful smile. "Son, that's one pretty lady."

Then he reached over and ruffled his son's hair. "Come on. Let's get you guys inside. It's getting chilly."

Returning from her classes near noon the next day, Jessica observed the mailman's jeep pulling away from her mailbox. Climbing from her car, she walked over to the tunnel-shaped receptacle which, like the others on her street, was set on a post next to the road. Jessie rifled through its contents. Good, her dividend check had arrived. She could buy that book she still needed for her Shakespeare class. Looking up she noticed a woman at the Bennington mailbox.

"Lovely day, isn't it?" The woman smiled. She was slightly portly, sixtyish, and her dark hair was liberally streaked with gray. She had a friendly air about her.

"Yes it is," replied Jessica. "It's nice to see the sun after our rainy winter."

"I'm Agatha, Mr. Bennington's housekeeper." She walked over to Jessica.

Jessie introduced herself.

"I understand that you rescued Smokey yesterday. That makes you 'A-number-one' in Becky's book."

Agatha, too, welcomed her to the neighborhood. She was sure Jessie would enjoy it here, she said. The neighbors were pleasant, and the neighborhood was quiet with the houses so widely spaced.

Jessica told her she loved the countryish atmosphere, which was becoming harder and harder to find in this rapidly developing area.

They both looked up as David Bennington walked out of the house and came towards them. He wore a suit and tie, and as he drew closer, Jessie couldn't help thinking that he was even better looking in the daylight. He was undoubtedly one of the handsomest men she'd ever met. She felt a long-forgotten stir within her which she immediately quashed. Never again, Jessica, she told herself. Besides, he's a married man. The conveniently safe circumstances pleased her.

"I was just telling Jessica a little about the neighborhood," Agatha told him.

"I think we should also warn her to expect a visitor this afternoon," he said, smiling at Jessica. "After you left last night, Becky began making a gift for you. To thank you for finding Smokey. I believe she intends to deliver it this afternoon."

"I'll look forward to it," Jessica assured him. "And how sweet of her to think of giving me a gift." The child's thoughtfulness touched her. The Benningtons and Agatha were all very nice, and they had made her feel welcome.

Then David turned to Agatha. "I've got to leave now, Agatha. Could you make me a quick sandwich to go? I have a meeting in an hour. I'll eat on the road."

"Of course," Agatha replied warmly. It was apparent that she was fond of her employer. "Good-bye, Jessica," she said, giving Jessie's arm a light touch. "We'll be seeing a lot of you, I'm sure." Agatha and David Bennington walked home together, obviously comfortable in each other's company.

As Jessica watched them leave, she wondered what Mrs. Bennington was like and why she hadn't met her yet.

Walking towards the house she saw another car stop at a mailbox across the street. Jessie observed an attractive woman in a tennis skirt and jacket gathering her mail. The woman looked her way, and Jessica waved.

The woman walked toward her. "You just bought the Brower place, right?" They introduced themselves.

Her name was Pat. She was petite, fit-looking, and perhaps a few years older than Jessica's twenty-six years. They chatted for a bit about the chaos of moving, and then Jessie asked Pat where she played tennis.

"At Woodsborough Swim and Tennis Club, just up the road. Do you play?"

"I played in high school, and my husband and I used to play mixed doubles occasionally with friends." Pat suggested that perhaps Jessica would like to fill in sometime when their group needed an extra.

"I'd love to," Jessie replied.

They heard a car coming then and moved closer to the side of the road. David Bennington was apparently leaving for his meeting. As he drove by, all three waved.

"Have you met the Benningtons?" Pat asked.

Jessica replied that she'd met David, the children, and Agatha, but that she hadn't met Mrs. Bennington yet.

"Cassandra doesn't live with the family anymore," Pat explained, a hint of coolness tingeing her voice. "She and David divorced a couple of years ago."

"And he has custody of the children?"

"Yes. Cassandra's in law school now, and apparently the family cramps her style." An uncomfortable pause followed, and Jessica, guessing that Pat didn't care to discuss the Benningtons' marital status further, dropped the subject.

"Well, David, Agatha, and the children all seem very nice."

"They are. David's a wonderful father and a great

guy. He and my husband play a lot of tennis together. And all three children are genuinely nice kids. Tad and my son, Josh, are best friends."

Then, promising to call Jessie for tennis soon, Pat departed.

As Jessica turned to go inside, she couldn't help stopping for a moment to admire her new home. The cream-colored, wood siding set off the black shutters nicely, she thought, and the two bay windows gave it a homey touch. She was becoming fond of sitting on the padded bench within and sipping her morning coffee. As she ascended the wooden steps that led to a small front porch, she made a mental note to fill its long wooden planter with flowers the first chance she got.

Entering the house, she dropped her books on the kitchen table. Two of her instructors had given extensive reading assignments for tomorrow, so she knew how she'd be spending this afternoon. Actually she didn't mind the work; it felt kind of nice to be back in school again.

She had interrupted her education at the end of her junior year of college so that she and Jim could get married. She'd worked to support them both while Jim finished his education, intending to go back to school when Jim had a job.

And then Jim died.

She had felt so desperately alone. If only she'd had

Jim's baby. At least she would feel she still had a part of him.

But thanks to his intelligence and foresight, she at least didn't have any immediate financial worries. He'd joined a small engineering firm in Silicon Valley after finishing school. In the few short years he'd been with them, the company did well, and Jim's stock options had grown into a nice nest egg. That, combined with his life insurance, had enabled Jessica to buy this house and to plan to finish her education.

Now, after a quick sandwich, she moved to the living room and settled into a chair for an afternoon of reading.

The following week, early on a Saturday afternoon as Jessica sat studying on the back patio, taking advantage of the warm spring sunshine, she heard her doorbell ring. "I'm in the backyard," she called out. She hadn't quite managed to pull herself out of the lounge chair when Becky came walking along the side of the house, with her latest kindergarten art project in hand.

"Want to see what we did at school yesterday?" She proudly displayed a swirly watercolor painting.

Jessica listened to a detailed explanation of the painting and admired it at length before pulling herself out of the chair. "I was just going to take a break and have some orange juice. It's freshly squeezed from the oranges on my tree, would you like some?"

This was Becky's third visit this week. The first had been to bring Jessica's reward for rescuing Smokey— another multi-colored watercolor painting. The last time, she had brought a crayon drawing. To Becky's delight, Jessie had put them up on her refrigerator with magnets.

They were sipping their juice and watching a gray squirrel romp through the grass, attempting to coax it to themselves with a walnut, when David Bennington came walking towards them. He wore tennis shorts and a short-sleeved knit shirt. The well-developed muscles of his tanned arms strained at the knit cuffs of his shirt sleeves, and his stomach looked flat as a twenty-year-old's. Perspiration dampened the edges of his short dark hair.

Jessica's heart rate increased at the sight of him.

David approached them, and stood smiling indulgently at his daughter, shaking his head. "Agatha said I'd probably find you here." Then his eyes shifted to Jessica. "I hear a certain visitor has been calling upon you quite often lately."

As always, he looked into her eyes when he spoke, and once again she had to clamp down on inner stirrings of attraction to the man. This was getting ridiculous! She struggled to treat him casually, without appearing either flustered or aloof, and told him that she enjoyed Becky's visits.

"Becky," he said, looking back at his daughter,

"why don't you run on home. Agatha says Smokey's food dish is empty."

"Daddy . . ." she pleaded in her best cajoling voice.

"You heard me, Becky," he retorted with a gentle firmness.

Sighing loudly and then shrugging her shoulders, she ran off towards home.

His eyes came back to Jessica. "Mind if I sit down? I played tennis longer than I intended, and I'm bushed. Guess I'm out of shape after the wet winter we've had."

As he lowered himself into one of the chairs, Jessica noticed again his flat stomach and broad shoulders. *Out of shape, indeed*, she thought.

"Jessica," David continued, "I hope Becky's not making a nuisance of herself. She likes you very much, and Agatha's having a hard time keeping her from coming over here." He sat bent over towards her with his elbows on his knees, his hands clasped in front of him.

"You see," he continued, "Becky's mother no longer lives with us, and I guess Becky misses a feminine presence in the house. She goes to her friends' homes and sees . . ." He paused. "Well, you understand."

He watched her eyes soften in sympathy. Man, she was beautiful. Those large brown eyes and full sensuous lips. And her nose today was softly pink, perhaps from sitting out here in the sun.

"Yes, of course."

"Agatha's great," he continued, trying to keep his mind on what he was trying to say, "but she's older, more the grandmotherly type. It seems to make a difference. You've been very nice to Becky and she's warmed by that."

Jessica assured him that she enjoyed Becky's visits, and that if they became too frequent, she would explain to the little girl that she was busy. "But she's usually very quiet. She'll often color with her crayons silently if I have work to do." Her compassion for Becky had calmed her racing heart.

"What kind of work do you do?" he asked, reaching for one of her textbooks. He read the title. "*Handbook of Technical Writing.* Are you a technical writer?"

"A student right now. I have about two more quarters before I get my degree. I hope to be able to do some technical writing eventually."

"When you're ready, come see us. We're always looking for good technical writers."

When she questioned him, he explained that he was one of three founders of a small computer parts manufacturing company here in this area south of San Francisco known as Silicon Valley. She knew the area had grown from one or two small businesses, begun by graduates of Stanford University's Electrical Engineering and Physics departments in the 1930's, to a multi-billion-dollar high tech industry today. She also knew, from Jim's background in the field, that silicon was the name of the material used in the production of computer "chips."

Jessica was also familiar with the name of David's company and knew that it was reputed to be one of the more successful small manufacturers in the Valley.

"It must be very strenuous, getting a small business started. Do you have to spend a lot of hours at the office?"

"At times, yeah. I try to keep it down to a minimum now, though. Long hours are hard on a family."

Just then Becky came skipping along the side of the house towards the backyard. "Daddy, I have to ask you something. Agatha said . . ." She dropped her voice to a whisper and cupped his ear with her small hands.

"Becky, he protested, "you know whispering is rude." But he listened to what she said, the frown of mild irritation slowly disappearing from his face. Then he straightened and looked at her for a few seconds while she jumped up and down, clapping her hands and chirping, "Please, Daddy, please."

David tried to cover his annoyance. He wasn't sure this was a good idea. Becky really should bring questions like this up in private first. But now, what else could he do but assent without appearing rude?

"Yeah . . . sure . . . if she wants to."

Becky ran over to Jessica and with both hands gripping her forearm, jumped up and down again. "Agatha said you could have dinner with us if you want to. Say you want to, please, please, please."

Surprised, Jessie looked from Becky to her father.

David looked noncommittal at first, but then he raised his eyebrows and, with what she thought was a perfunctory smile, nodded once and assured her that Becky . . . all of them . . . would be happy if she'd join them. If she liked grilled hamburgers.

Then standing up, he glanced at his watch, "Is six o'clock all right?"

Unsure of what to do but unable to think of a reason to refuse, Jessica accepted their invitation, agreeing to be there by 6:00.

She watched as Becky and David walked towards their own house, Becky holding her father's hand and skipping. She turned back to wave at Jessie.

After they'd gone, Jessica considered calling to cancel the engagement. She picked up the phone twice, only to put it down again. She'd already committed herself, she decided, and they were all being so pleasant. However, the whole situation had the potential of causing her more disturbance and pain than she could handle right now.

And then there was the ridiculous way she was reacting to David.

When Jim died, she'd suffered terribly.

She decided that she would never allow herself to be hurt that way again, never allow herself to love that way again. She would cherish the memory of the devotion that she and Jim had shared, and it would always be a part of her. But now, it was time to move on to another area of fulfillment: a career. She enjoyed writing, and she was determined that writing would satisfy or fulfill her emotional needs from now on. Besides, writers needed solitude, and she possessed that in abundance now.

As for the Benningtons, she would go this time. But after today, she would make a decided effort to engross herself more in her work, perhaps spend more time at school.

Chapter Two

At 6:00, Jessie rang the Bennington doorbell. She carried a bouquet of spring flowers from her garden and a small bag of hard candy for the children. She had barely taken her finger off the bell when an excited Becky flung open the door.

"Hi! Come on in. Want to see my room and my doll house?"

"Becky, let Jessica catch her breath," Agatha said, coming up behind her and chuckling. "Why, what lovely flowers, Jessica. I'll bet they're from your garden."

"Yes. Mrs. Brower must have loved gardening. She left me so many pretty flowers."

"Well, I'm sure Lillian is happy that someone who appreciates them is taking care of them now," Agatha said, a softness coming into her eyes as she spoke of her previous neighbor. "She hated to leave her house, you know, poor dear. But after Victor died—that was Mr. Brower—it all became too much for her, what with her arthritis and all. I'm sure you know that she's gone to live with her daughter."

"Yes," Jessica replied. "I told her to come back and visit the old place anytime she likes. I hope she will."

She handed Becky the small bag of candy jawbreakers she'd gotten at the neighborhood grocery store that afternoon. "I don't know if kids still like these, but I used to love them."

"Oh boy," Becky exclaimed enthusiastically as she opened the bag and looked inside.

"Put them aside until after dinner, Becky," Agatha admonished gently.

Jessica looked up from her enjoyment of Becky's enthusiasm, to see that a young girl of about eleven or twelve years of age had joined them. She deduced that she must be another one of David's children for she had his brown hair and hazel eyes. The eyes, however, were somber and lacked the twinkle usually shown in David's.

Agatha walked over to the young girl and put her arm around her. "This is Becky's sister, Rachael. Rachael, this is our new neighbor, Jessica Roberts."

"It's nice to meet you." The young girl spoke softly and managed a half-hearted smile. She looked as though she'd been crying.

Grabbing Jessica's hand, Becky pulled her towards a hallway off the living room. "Okay, now come see my doll house. I just got a new kitchen table and stove."

Smiling at Agatha and Rachael, Jessica allowed herself to be pulled to Becky's room. On the way, she got a cursory look at a portion of the house. The living room, in which they'd been standing, was homey and warm and yet had an elegance about it. It had a high ceiling, a brick fireplace, and a comfortable-looking, overstuffed couch and two chairs. Walking down the hallway, they passed a boy's bedroom, obviously Tad's, with football pennants on the walls, a couple of trophies on a shelf, and a sports motif bedspread.

Becky pulled Jessica into her own room which contained light French provincial furniture and a canopied bed. It was a large sunny room with frilly curtains. The doll house was against one wall. Becky proceeded to take Jessica on a systematic, room-by-room inspection of the miniature house and its furniture. They had examined about half the rooms when they heard a door slam and voices in the outer portion of the house.

"Daddy and Tad are home," Becky said, looking up.

"Shall we go and say hello and see the rest of your doll house later?" Jessica asked.

"Okay." Becky jumped to her feet and out into the hallway before Jessica could unbend her legs and push herself up from the floor on which they'd both been sitting. As they walked through the living room and towards the kitchen, the voices became louder and more distinct.

They entered the kitchen to see David, Tad, Rachael, and Agatha. Tad was talking animatedly. ". . . right over the outfielder's head. I barely slid into home when . . ." He paused when Becky and Jessie came into the room. "Becky, I hit a home run!" He wore a baseball uniform, one leg of which was smeared with dirt. He went on to give them all another vivid description of his feat.

Jessica looked up at David who stood behind his son, his eyes crinkled in a patient smile. He looked down at Tad with obvious pride and warmth. He wore a short-sleeved, yellow knit polo shirt, open at the collar, and blue jeans.

As though he felt her scrutiny, he shifted his gaze to her. "Hello, Jessica. We've got a little excitement here."

"Yes, I see. Congratulations, Tad."

"Thanks."

The chill in his tone surprised her.

He returned to describing the game to his sisters and Agatha.

Jessica looked up to find David's gaze upon her again. The smile had faded from his eyes and his mouth tensed, becoming something between a smile and a grimace. His brows lifted over eyes that seemed to hold an apology for his son's rudeness.

He'd have to talk with Tad, David thought. He understood the boy's behavior: He was feeling hurt because his mother had been ignoring him lately. But that was no reason to take it out on the rest of the adult members of the female gender. When he'd seen the confused hurt in Jessica's eyes, he'd almost made an automatic move towards her. But what would he have done when he got there? Hastily, he diverted his mind to other matters.

"Okay, guys, let's get these hamburgers on the grill. I've still got work to do tonight."

Half an hour later, Jessica sat in a chair on the patio and watched as David flipped hamburgers with a spatula and bantered with his children. When he reached out to stroke Becky's blond curls, Jessica couldn't help musing that such large, masculine-looking hands could also be gentle as he touched his child.

When the hamburgers were done, they moved inside for dinner, a casual one at the round kitchen table. The spring evening, although unseasonably warm, was still too cool to enable them to eat outside comfortably. When they sat down, Jessie experienced both delight and apprehension at finding herself sitting next to David.

She enjoyed the chatter and laughter around the dinner table. As she listened and occasionally entered the conversation, however, she found her gaze constantly returning to David. When he spoke, she watched him, noticing the healthy bronze tan of his face; the animated eyes, warm and teasing; the strength implicit in his smoothly shaved jaw line.

Suddenly, she realized he was looking back at her, and she quickly tore her gaze away, flushing with embarrassment.

Why did this man interest her so? She hardly knew him. No one but Jim had ever claimed her constant attention before.

Then, thankfully, Tad began telling a story of an amusing incident at school and everyone turned to listen. Grateful for the distraction, Jessica strove to concentrate on what he said.

But after a few minutes, as she listened to Tad's animated monologue, Jessica realized that another, quieter conversation had begun between David and Rachael, who sat on his other side. Before she realized she had eavesdropped, she heard him ask a question in a low voice. "Is she coming?"

"She said she'd try," the girl replied, and Jessica observed that her young eyes had again filled with tears. She also noticed that Rachael had taken only a few bites of her hamburger.

Jessica couldn't help scrutinizing David's expression. She saw that his jaw had set in a rigid line. His eyes, just a few moments before so warm and animated, had turned cold.

Then Agatha's voice distracted her. "Since we have a guest tonight," Agatha suggested, "why don't we have dessert in the living room."

The children noisily assented, and they all adjourned to the next room. Jessica helped Agatha to slice the still warm apple pie and then to carry it, along with plates, coffee, and milk, out to the living room.

They had just begun to eat their dessert when they heard the front door open and then slam shut. From the foyer, an extremely attractive blond woman entered the room. She wore pale blue slacks and a matching oversized sweater. Her hair, tied casually at the nape of her neck, and her subtle but expertly applied makeup gave her an appearance of understated elegance. But she had a cool look in her eyes, and her attitude implied boredom.

Becky jumped up. "Hi, Mommy!" She ran to her and hugged the neck the woman briefly lowered to her.

The other children rose and greeted her also, but with less enthusiasm.

Then Jessica noticed the look on David's face: He was glaring at his ex-wife. His eyes had gone icy cold, and again his jaw line set rigidly. He put down his fork and, elbows on his knees, clasped his hands together so tightly that the muscles in his forearms became clearly defined.

After kissing each child on the head or cheek—perfunctorily, rather than warmly, Jessica noted—her eyes scanned the room. She nodded at Agatha. Her "Hello, David," was delivered in a flat monotone.

Then her gaze moved to Jessica. When David introduced them, Jessica thought she saw a glint of amused interest as the woman's eyes flickered to David and then back to Jessie again.

So this was Cassandra.

She had barely acknowledged the introduction when she turned to address Rachael, again speaking in an emotionless monotone. "Okay, Rachael, let's go see what you've got."

Jessie saw David and Agatha exchange glances. Agatha's eyes looked sad, but David's reflected cold steel.

Becky watched her mother and sister leave the room. "Did Rachael find a new dress for her graduation?" she asked. David nodded. "Can I go see too?"

Again David nodded assent. "Sure, go ahead."

After Becky had left, a long uncomfortable silence filled the room, during which Jessie felt like an unwelcome intruder. The six plates of apple pie sat practically untouched and getting cold.

Finally, with a deep sigh, David seemed to remember Jessica's presence. In a voice devoid of emotion, he explained to her that Cassandra had come to give Rachael an opinion on two junior-high graduation dresses which the child and Agatha had brought home from the store on approval. "Cassandra didn't have time to go shopping with Rachael," he explained, "but she's apparently not pleased with the description of the dresses that Rachael gave her. She's bringing a . . . special friend . . . to the exercises and wants Rachael to look just right." Then running his hand through his hair, he got up and began to pace the floor.

Tad sat silently with a shuttered look in his eyes, throwing his baseball into his mitt.

Soon Cassandra came breezing back into the room. "Agatha, take her to return those dresses. Honestly, they're positively dowdy. I'll try to clear some time to take her shopping one day next week."

"Look, Cassandra, Agatha was only . . ." David began in an agitated voice. Then he seemed to think better of arguing with her. He paused for a moment, took a deep breath, and appeared to calm his emotions. He looked at Rachael who had followed Cassandra back into the room. "Is that all right with you, honey?"

"It's fine, Daddy," Rachael nodded. Her attempt to smile was not entirely successful.

"Now I have to run," Cassandra announced, "I have an appointment this evening." She issued a general good-bye and headed for the door. They heard it slam behind her.

"Mom, I hit a home run today," Tad mumbled sarcastically, looking at the floor. Then he threw his glove down next to the chair and left the room, heading towards his bedroom.

"Let's play a game," the undaunted Becky proposed. Agatha pleaded fatigue and letters to write. She gathered up the plates of apple pie, saying she would put them aside until later. No one objected.

Jessica, feeling uncomfortable, declared an intention

to leave. Rachael and Becky pleaded with her to stay, however, "for just one game." She agreed—just one. As they began to set up the game board, Jessica noticed David leave the room and head in the direction that Tad had disappeared.

The three played the game for about an hour, during which time David and Tad drifted in and out of the room.

When they'd finished the game, Jessica announced that she really must go home. Becky protested again, but David reminded her that it was past her bedtime. He ordered her off to get ready for bed and then offered to walk Jessica home.

As they stepped out into the cool night air, Jessica pulled her sweater more closely around her. Despite the warmth of the day, the night had turned cool.

As they approached the end of the Bennington driveway and turned right towards Jessie's house, she tried to make conversation by admiring the countless stars in the sky; so many more were visible out here, away from the lights of any big city. Obviously preoccupied, David glanced up at the sky without commenting. Another moment of silence followed, then he spoke quietly.

"I'm sorry, Jessica. Cassandra's visit must have made you uncomfortable."

"It's all right. Everyone has problems," she responded.

He lapsed into silence again.

She glanced up at his rugged profile as he walked beside her. The moonlight shone on his dark hair and high cheekbones. His attitude was somber. The thought struck her that since Cassandra's visit, he hardly seemed the same open, cheerful person anymore. Now he seemed to have erected an emotional barricade around himself. She began to have some perception of the prodigious load he carried all alone: the responsibilities of both his business and his family. She experienced an overwhelming desire to comfort him somehow.

They arrived at her door. She unlocked it, turned the kitchen light on, and stepped inside.

He stood in the doorway and squinted in the light. His eyes took in the room. "Well, looks like you're pretty well settled." His mouth formed a tentative smile, but his eyes remained somber.

"Good night, Jessica. Again, I'm sorry."

For some reason, which she couldn't explain, his cheerless attitude distressed her. She looked at him with a mixture of anxiety and sympathy. "Please, don't worry on my account. I understand how these things can be. Really." She tried to inject the sincerity she felt into her words, perhaps to make him feel better in some small way.

His dark eyes looked into hers. "You're a nice person, Jessica." Her sincerity moved him. It warmed, a little, the self-protective coldness that Cassandra always aroused in him. When he said good night, he realized that he did so reluctantly.

After David had left, Jessica tried to put him out of her mind. Nevertheless, the feelings he had evoked in her that evening kept creeping into her consciousness: both the constant awareness and the compassionate concern. Perhaps she shouldn't have gone over there after all. She redoubled her resolve to engross herself in her work hereafter.

A week later, late on Sunday morning, Jessica sat at her computer, drinking coffee and typing. Except for a visit from Becky yesterday morning, she had done almost nothing but study since Friday afternoon. She was working on a paper that comprised a large percentage of her grade in one class, and she wanted it to be good. But oh, she thought, it would be nice to have someone to talk to for just a little while. I could use a break.

True to her resolve, she had spent many additional hours at school during the past week, but Becky had nevertheless caught her at home several times. She found herself reluctantly growing fond of the little girl.

She hadn't seen David, however, since last Saturday evening when he had walked her home. She'd learned from Becky that he had been out of town on business for much of the week.

The poignancy of the feelings he'd evoked in her had faded somewhat during the intervening time, much to her relief; although, once or twice, she found herself looking up hopefully while working in her front yard and hearing a car pass by. And during one of Becky's visits, she thought she'd heard his step on the path alongside her house, coming to fetch Becky.

Jessica had also gotten to know Pat a little better over the past week. Pat had called one day to say that their fourth for tennis doubles wasn't feeling well and would Jessica like to fill in. Jessie had gone gladly, and although she had started out a little shakily, her game slowly improved. She had enjoyed the morning. But since getting home from that tennis game, she'd done very little but study.

As Jessica now reread the last paragraph she'd typed, the telephone rang.

"Hi Jessie, it's Pat. Would you, by any chance, be up for a little tennis again?"

Jessie explained that she had a paper to finish by tomorrow, but that she'd just been feeling the need for a little break. She could play for an hour or so.

"My husband, Brad, and David went up to the club looking for a doubles game a little while ago, but there's no one around. They called to see if I could find another woman for some mixed doubles. How about it?"

David? Oh, no! Jessie wished she could take back her acceptance of Pat's invitation, but she knew that would appear rude. Besides, she wanted Pat to continue to ask her to play. With women friends. She'd go, but only for the hour she promised. What harm could one hour do? She resolved to completely block from her mind any undesired effect of David's presence.

"Sure, that sounds like fun," Jessie replied, trying to sound enthusiastic.

"Good. I'll pick you up in about ten minutes."

Jessica got out a pair of white shorts and a yellow tank top. She supposed these would do. She'd worn the only tennis skirt she had on Friday, and it was soiled. If I'm going to play tennis occasionally now, I'd better get another skirt or two, she thought.

She had just finished adding a little makeup and gotten her tennis racquet out of the closet when she heard Pat's car horn.

As they entered the tennis club, Jessie noticed that only two of the six tennis courts were occupied. Her attention flew immediately to one on which two men stood at the net, talking. One of them was David. Both men looked up as the women entered the tennis court gate.

"Hello, Jessica," David gave her a slow smile, and his eyes held hers. After a brief moment, she looked away.

Pat introduced her to Brad. "Hi, Jessica! Glad Pat could talk you into joining us." He was a pleasant-looking man, about David's age, Jessie guessed—in his mid-thirties. He had sandy-brown hair and wore wire-rimmed glasses.

"Come on, Jessica. Let's take them on," David exclaimed.

She started out playing shakily again. She and David lost the first four games because of her missed shots. She gradually started to improve, however, and although they lost the first set, the score was a respectable four to six.

"Okay, here's our strategy for the next set," David said, smiling. With his hand on the back of her neck and then sliding to her opposite shoulder, he turned her away from Brad and Pat and walked her several steps away.

She didn't hear a word he said. He had pulled her close and his face was just a few inches from her own as he whispered his plan. She looked into his tanned face and could see a light film of perspiration on his forehead. Her heart beat rapidly. Pulling away from him, she nodded an acknowledgment of the plan she hadn't heard.

She wasn't sure how, but she and David won the second set of games by a narrow margin.

Then Brad suggested playing a third set, but Jessica was relieved to be able to legitimately decline. After all, she had said just an hour, and they'd already played longer than that.

"I'm sorry, but I have an important paper due tomorrow. I'd better get home and back to work on it," she explained.

"You two go ahead and play some singles if you

like," David offered. I'll take Jessica home. I'd better get back to my family too, especially since I have to be out of town again all next week."

Jessica made polite conversation on the way home, to keep her mind off her recent reaction to David's closeness. "Do you travel on business a lot?"

"Not any more." he replied. "I try to keep it down to just a few days every couple of months, especially now since the kids have essentially only one parent around." She saw his jaw tighten. "This week and next are kind of a special circumstance and can't be helped."

They pulled into her driveway.

"Thank you for bringing me home," Jessica said when the car stopped in front of her door. "That was fun. I started out kind of shakily, but I'm glad we won one set."

He put his hand out to shake hers, "Nice going, partner." They clasped hands. "And good luck with your paper." He smiled into her eyes.

"Thank you." He continued to hold her hand, and she couldn't bring herself to pull it away. "Say hello to the children and Agatha for me."

"I will." His smile faded, but he continued looking into her eyes. An intensity entered his expression. Then slowly it eased, and he loosened his hold. She hesitantly withdrew her hand from his and got out of the car.

Once inside, Jessica found it difficult to concentrate

on her paper. She kept remembering the feel of David's touch on her shoulder and the delicious confusion she'd felt at being pulled so close to him during their game. And then in the car when he'd held her hand, she'd thought for a moment that he was going to kiss her.

Stop it, Jessica! she admonished herself. She realized that in order to put a halt to this, she'd have to try to avoid him completely, even if it meant being rude sometimes. To strengthen her resolve she forced herself to remember the pain of loss she'd felt after Jim's death and the vulnerability at finding herself unable to earn her own living. She vowed anew to concentrate solely on her studies and on the development of a career. Sobered, and with a new determination, she returned to work.

The final version of Jessica's paper turned out well, and she was relieved to finally hand it in and forget about it. Another assignment waited in the wings, however: the first rough draft of a project for her technical writing class. The class was assigned the cooperative task of designing a potential new computer classroom. The school actually planned to construct a new classroom of this type and was prepared to seriously consider any suggestions and ideas the students offered.

The class divided into groups, and Jessica's group, which consisted of herself and two young men, had the assignment of creating the environmental design. They had to consider the size of the room; lighting; ventilation: windows vs. air conditioning; organization of computer workstations; and types of computer stands or tables.

Last week, Jessica had had an appointment to view a computer classroom at Stanford University and to discuss possible workstation layouts with one of the instructors. The young woman had been very helpful and had even provided Jessica with various diagrams which she had obtained at a recent conference.

On Wednesday, Jessica worked all evening and well into the night, organizing her material which was due the following morning. She was pleased with the result, and hoped for a good grade.

On Thursday afternoon when she returned from class, the tension of her report out of the way, she felt ravenous. Deciding to prepare her favorite chicken recipe, she assembled the ingredients. Halfway through her preparation of the dish, Jessica realized that she didn't have any of the cheese she needed.

She wondered if Pat or Agatha had some. She dialed Pat's number but was greeted by her answering machine. Agatha answered the Bennington phone, however, and said that yes, she indeed did have the kind of cheese that Jessica needed, and she was welcome to it.

"I'll be right over," Jessica told her.

A vociferous Becky greeted her at the Bennington front door. "We're having hot chocolate!"

When they entered the kitchen, two cups of hot chocolate stood on the table. Rachael sat behind one of them with her hands wrapped around the mug. Becky climbed onto the other chair and began sipping at the other. Poor Rachael looked upset again.

"We're trying to comfort Rachael with some hot chocolate," Agatha explained. "She's still having graduation dress problems. Her mother had to cancel another shopping date with her."

"My graduation is next week! I'll never get another dress in time." Rachael's voice held a hint of panic.

"I'm reluctant to go shopping again with Rachael," Agatha said. "Mrs. Bennington didn't like my selection at all the last time."

Jessica thought for a moment. It couldn't do any harm for her to help Rachael. Rachael was too grown up to arouse the kind of yearning that Becky often did. And she knew how important the right clothes could be for a girl Rachael's age. The child looked so distraught.

"Can I help?" she finally asked. "I could go with you tomorrow after school. We could at least look. What do we have to lose?"

Rachael looked up hopefully and glanced from Jessica to Agatha and back to Jessica again. Her face creased into a tentative smile. "You wouldn't mind?" she asked.

"Not at all. It will be fun!"

She got the directions to Rachael's school and arranged to pick her up at 3 o'clock the following afternoon.

Then she gathered up her cheese and returned to her own kitchen.

After dinner, thinking she should have some idea of what young girls wore these days before going shopping with Rachael, she went into town and purchased a *Seventeen* magazine. Thumbing through it after returning home, she saw several styles that would look lovely on a young girl Rachael's age.

Chapter Three

The next afternoon at 3 o'clock, Jessica parked in front of Rachael's school, watching students stream out of the doors. She spotted Rachael and waved.

The girl waved back, ran towards the car, and got inside. She smiled and seemed happier than Jessica had ever seen her in the few times they'd been together.

"Where would you like to go first?" Jessie asked. Rachael named a popular department store, and they set off.

They found one or two possibilities at the first store but decided to look further.

At the second store, most of the dresses had too many frills for Rachael's taste, and they found themselves giggling as Rachael strutted around the small dressing room in the exaggerated styles.

At the third store, Rachael found just the dress she'd been looking for. Its subtle, pastel print was of a soft, flowing fabric, and the style seemed perfect. Making sure they could return the dress if it didn't meet with her family's approval, they bought it. Rachael beamed.

Then Jessica noticed some tennis clothes in the next department. Looking through them, she selected a skirt. Rachael helped her find a top to match. Jessica bought them both.

They stopped for ice-cream sodas on the way home. As Rachael smiled and chattered between sips on her straw, Jessica found herself thinking that Rachael was really a very attractive girl. With her dark hair and hazel eyes, she resembled David a great deal.

She could tell that Rachael had begun to feel comfortable with her, and Jessica was beginning to like Rachael very much. She sensed that the child was capable of a great deal of spirit and enthusiasm. She wondered why she had seen so little of it until now.

Late the following afternoon as Jessica sat at her kitchen table studying, the doorbell rang. The day was warm and the kitchen window was open. Jessica could hear Becky's voice outside.

Opening her door, she was surprised to see Rachael there too. Becky jumped up and down. "Rachael wants to ask you something." Letting them in and closing the door, Jessica turned to Rachael.

"I want to invite you to my graduation," Rachael told her, an excitement in her voice. "I hope you can come. It's next Thursday night at seven o'clock, and then we're all coming back to our house for punch and cake. My mother and my grandma and grandpa are coming too."

Surprised, Jessica wasn't sure how to respond. "Gee, I don't know. I mean it . . . it . . . sounds like a family party."

She thought of David. If she went, she'd have to see him. But if his wife were there too, he'd probably be preoccupied. Perhaps seeing them together might even cure Jessica of this ridiculous infatuation she had developed for him.

"Agatha's coming too," Rachael encouraged hopefully; however, the enthusiasm in her voice had become more subdued and her smile faded.

"Does your father know you've invited me?"

"He's not home from Boston yet, but I know he'll say it's okay. He's coming home tonight."

"Why don't you talk it over with your dad. If he says it's all right, I'd love to come," Jessica told her, wanting to see the smile back on her face and in her eyes again.

"Oh good! I'll know he'll say it's okay. We'll let you know about the time and everything." Her smile was back.

"Maybe you can ride with us," Becky chimed in.

* * *

The following morning, Jessica drove to campus early to do some library research for an assigned paper in her Shakespeare class. It was mid-afternoon before she got back to Woodsborough.

As she turned into her own street, she looked in the rearview mirror. Another car had also turned in behind her. Looking more closely, she saw that it was David. Without thinking, she waved into the rearview mirror. He must have been watching, because he waved back. When she pulled into her driveway, he pulled in behind her.

Getting out of her car, she gathered up her books and waited as he approached. "Welcome back," she greeted him. "Did you have a nice trip?"

"We accomplished a lot, but it was tiring." He wore a dress shirt with sleeves rolled to his mid-forearms. The top button of his shirt was open and his tie loosened. He looked tired.

"I want to thank you, Jessica, for taking Rachael shopping for her graduation dress. That was very nice of you and beyond the call of duty."

Uh oh, she thought. Maybe he thought she'd interfered.

"When Mrs. Bennington had to cancel their shopping date," Jessica explained, "Rachael seemed concerned that she wouldn't be able to get a dress before Thursday. I hope it was all right that I took her."

"It was more than all right. You've made Rachael

happy. And we all like the dress very much." He spoke quietly, as if with fatigue, but there was a gentle warmth in his eyes despite the weariness she saw. She had a sudden, unexplainable urge to smooth with her fingers the lines of fatigue around his eyes.

In order to distract herself, she asked a question. "Has Mrs. Bennington seen the dress? I hope she likes it too."

The gentleness left his eyes, replaced by a sternness. "It seems to me that Mrs. Bennington has forfeited her right to an opinion," he said coldly.

A car went by the house just then and, although Jessica didn't recognize the occupant, David waved. When he looked back at her, his sternness had evaporated. "Rachael told me that she'd invited you to her graduation exercises and party. We hope you can come."

Jessica hesitated. "I'd like to come if I won't be interfering in a family party."

"It's Rachael's party, and she'd like very much for you to be there." After a few seconds, he added, "We'd all like you to come."

"Then I'd like to, very much."

Aware of his obvious weariness, to her own horror, she suddenly heard herself say, "You look tired. Would you like to come in for some iced tea or something?"

He opened his mouth to speak and from the look on his face she thought he was going to accept; but then he closed his mouth and began again. "I can't, Jessica; I'd better get home. I haven't spent much time with the kids in the past two weeks."

"I understand," she told him, relieved. Why in the world had she invited him in?

But then he reached out and touched her upper arm lightly. "But, please, ask me again." He began backing towards his car. "We'll pick you up at about six-fifteen on Thursday if that's all right."

"Fine," Jessica called back. "I'll be ready."

Jessica dressed with some trepidation the evening of Rachael's graduation exercises. Choosing a light jade-colored skirt and matching shell top, she topped it off with a muted plaid blazer, a combination that was an old standby favorite.

As she dressed, she wondered what was in store for her emotionally that night. What would it be like to have his Cassandra with them all evening? She wondered if David's hostility toward his ex-wife the night she'd come to see Rachael's dress was usual. She remembered the sadness in his eyes when he'd spoken of long working hours and their negative effect on a family. She guessed she'd gain more insight into the relationships of this family tonight. She had just finished putting on loop earrings and applying a little makeup when the doorbell rang.

When David looked down at her, his heart did a flip. She looked wonderful. She had a casual elegance about her that said she hadn't spent a lot of time on her appearance and yet looked like a million bucks. The first word that popped into his head was class: the woman exuded it. He suddenly wished his car wasn't loaded with other people, even if they were his own family. And yet, deep down, he knew it was for the best that they were there.

David ushered Jessica to the family wagon. The three children sat inside, along with Agatha and an elderly gentleman. Jessie slid into the second row of seats with Agatha, and smiled at the children in the back. David introduced the elderly gentleman in the front passenger seat as his father. The man had a full head of white hair and a cheerful aspect. He seemed genuinely happy to meet Jessica.

"The children can't stop talking about you," he told her.

Jessie absently wondered where the grandmother was.

Then her eyes sought out Rachael. She looked lovely in her new dress, and Jessica told her so. The young girl beamed with happiness. "We make a good shopping team."

When they entered the auditorium where the exercises were held, Rachael left them to sit with the other graduates. Because they'd come early, the rest of the party found seats near the front. Jessica seated herself between Becky and Agatha, and David sat at the end of the row near his father and Tad.

Once settled, Jessie strained to see Rachael, who now stood near the front of the auditorium with her fellow graduates. She couldn't help smiling. Rachael seemed the prettiest girl there as she chatted happily with her classmates.

Jessica sensed David looking at her. Their eyes met, and they both smiled, happy for Rachael.

Then his gaze seemed to slide past her, and his smile faded. Jessica turned to see Cassandra enter their row from the opposite aisle. A handsome man—a little too carefully handsome for Jessica's tastes—accompanied her, along with an elderly woman.

"Hi, Grandma! Hi, Mommy!" Becky chirped. The elderly woman sat next to Becky, who seemed genuinely pleased to see her. "This is Jessica. She lives next door to us. She found Smokey when he was lost, and she helped Rachael find her graduation dress."

The elderly woman's smile faltered, but she acknowledged Jessica with a pleasant nod.

"How good of you, Jessica," Cassandra injected dryly. She turned to her friend. "Derek, I believe you know everyone except David's friend, Jessica."

Jessica's face flushed, not knowing how David would feel at having responsibility for her presence attributed solely to him. Becky, however, came to the rescue. "Jessica's all of us's friend," she announced, not getting the phrase quite right, but making her meaning clear.

When Rachael went up to the podium to receive her

diploma, Becky climbed onto Jessica's lap in order to see better. When Rachael returned to her seat, she watched for a few more moments then turned to Jessie and snuggled into her lap. After a while, she began to doze. Jessica cuddled her and smoothed her hair.

She suddenly realized that the child no longer evoked the feeling of loss within her. Rather, she found that she enjoyed holding her and was developing a deep affection for her. She couldn't help wondering, however, if permitting herself these feelings might cause her pain at some future time.

Afterwards, back at the house, Jessica sat with her cake and punch, feeling out of place. She had helped Agatha set out the refreshments, but now that was finished, and she had no other excuse to keep busy.

Thankfully, after a few minutes, Rachael began opening her gifts. She seemed to like the miniature graduation hat that Jessica gave her for her charm bracelet. Her gift from Cassandra was a beautiful watch. Jessica glanced at David when Rachael opened it, but his expression betrayed nothing of his feelings.

When the last gift had been opened and conversation resumed, Jessica prepared to leave. The evening was still young, but she'd satisfied Rachael's desire to have her attend the festivities. Now she was beginning to feel out of place among these people who knew each other so well.

Before she could make a move, however, Cassandra announced that she and Derek had to leave. They had another engagement. Grandma could stay if David would bring her home later. Jessica watched Rachael's face fall at her mother's declaration. And as Cassandra retrieved her purse and jacket, Jessica noticed an angry scowl on Tad's face. When his mother leaned over to give the girls a good-bye peck on the cheek, the young boy escaped the room.

After the door had closed behind them, and Cassandra and Derek sauntered toward their car, Becky stood in the window, waving good-bye. But the two adults outside, already involved in their own conversation, never saw her.

An uncomfortable silence followed their departure. Then Grandpa, with characteristic cheerfulness, suggested a game.

Jessica couldn't leave now, even though she had several school assignments waiting for her attention at home. She couldn't further dampen Rachael's day.

She joined the family for a game of charades, and eventually Tad returned to join them. Soon they were laughing at each other's dramatics, the disappointment of Cassandra's early departure temporarily forgotten. Grandpa proved to have a wonderful sense of humor, and Tad, standoffish with Jessica until now, warmed and even became friendly and enthusiastic towards her. He told her that he liked the dress she had helped Rachael pick out.

When all began to tire of the game, Jessica decided that she really must leave. She had an unfinished assignment due in an early morning class. She helped the children put away the pads and pencils used in the game, then said her good-byes, thanking Rachael and David for including her in the day.

"I'll walk you home," David offered. When she started to protest, he insisted that he'd like some fresh air. "Besides, beautiful women shouldn't go walking around alone in the dark." He gave her a subtle but intimate smile, and Jessica couldn't help the pleasure that flowed through her at the compliment.

On the way home, they talked about the graduation exercises and laughed at some of the children's antics in their game of charades. Jessica also told David that she enjoyed getting to know his father.

But buried beneath Jessica's gaiety was a growing concern that she was becoming too engrossed in this family's life. Spending too much time with them and growing too fond of them. She had her own responsibilities and her own priorities, and she couldn't afford to ignore them. As a result of her musings, she realized that her manner had grown subdued.

When they reached her front door, she thanked David for walking her home. Opening the door, she stepped inside, and turned to say good night. But David had taken a step inside too, and when she looked up at him, saw that he watched her somberly.

"Is something wrong, Jessica?"

"No, I'm just tired, and I still have a lot of reading

to do tonight." She refused to let his eyes hold hers and dropped her gaze to the floor.

Then she felt his finger beneath her chin, raising her face to his. "That never kept your smile away before." His voice rumbled with gentleness, and his eyes—now that he'd forced her to look into them—seemed sincerely puzzled. She couldn't pull her gaze away this time.

His thumb moved slowly over her cheek, and the questioning in his eyes softened into a warmth which, despite her attempt to ignore it, seemed to spread through her too. The next moment, his thumb softly brushed her lips, and his mouth moved closer to hers. When their lips touched, a fire spread through her. Her knees went weak, and she wanted nothing more than to be taken into his arms.

But he drew back, and when she opened her eyes, smiled into them. "Thank you for coming today, Jessica," he whispered. "And thank you for all you've done for Rachael."

"It was my pleasure." She felt too numb to say more.

He stepped to the door and opened it. "Good night." He stood looking at her for a moment and then turned and left.

She trembled as she walked to the living room and sank into the sofa. She could still feel his kiss on her mouth and the vehemence of her reaction to him appalled her. In the next moment, she would have melted into his arms. His kiss was obviously only a gesture of gratitude, nothing more.

This has gone far enough, she told herself. It has to stop. I won't go over there anymore. And I'll spend most of my waking hours at school from now on.

During the following week, Jessica spent as much time at school as possible. She took a bag lunch with her or ate in the school cafeteria. She studied in the library. Most days she didn't come home until after dark. She tried to keep constantly busy to prevent herself from thinking about David and his family. She'd been letting them become far too important in her life. She needed other friends, other interests.

On Friday afternoon, after a late class, she joined some classmates for an early dinner and a movie. Afterwards they went out for coffee. As she sipped at her steaming cup, Jessica had trouble keeping her mind on the conversation going on around her.

She found herself wondering if Becky had been coming to the house; she pictured the little girl, disappointed and puzzled at her absence. A pang of guilt pricked at her. She had to admit that she missed seeing Becky very much. And Rachael. She wondered if Rachael had signed up for those tennis lessons she'd considered taking.

Jessica arrived home late.

As she unlocked her door and opened it, a swift movement at her feet startled her. Then something swished by her. She looked up to see Smokey scurry through the kitchen, into the living room, and onto her sofa. Laughing, she closed the door.

She walked to the living room and picked him up. He didn't protest being held this time and seemed to snuggle close. Jessica wondered how long he'd been out in the chill night air. As she cuddled and petted him, she found tears stinging her eyes. She'd even missed this silly cat.

Looking up at the clock, she saw that it was 10:45. Rather late, but she'd better call, just in case Becky was awake and upset. She dialed the number, still holding Smokey.

"Hello." It was David voice, soft and low.

"David, it's Jessica." In the pause that followed, she steeled herself against the soft feelings any contact with him provoked. It seemed ages ago since she'd last talked to him.

"Jessica." Another pause. "Where have you been all week? Becky's been looking for you."

"I've been very busy at school." It was the truth, she told herself. "Listen, the reason I'm calling is that I have a lost kitten here. Are you missing one?"

He laughed. "We sure are. I just got Becky to sleep. She's been so worried about him. I think she's gone over to your house four or five times this evening, looking for him. And you."

Jessica felt another pang of guilt. "I can keep

Smokey here tonight, if you like, and bring him home in the morning."

"No need for that. I'll come over and get him."

Her heart leaped to her throat. No! She didn't want to be alone with him. She opened her mouth to protest, but before she could say anything, he'd hung up the phone.

Five minutes later, a light knock sounded at her door. Her heart thumped with resolve as she went to answer it. She would return the cat and be done with it.

When she opened the door, his presence hit her with a force that took her breath away. He was big and handsome and smelled of his now familiar after-shave. Jessica experienced a roller-coaster-like dip in the pit of her stomach and had to make a conscious effort to steady her voice as she spoke.

"Come in, David. He's here somewhere. He scurried off towards the back rooms. I'll get him."

She glanced only briefly into the two smaller rooms on her way towards her own bedroom at the end of the hall; she was pretty sure that's where he'd gone. Each of the smaller rooms still contained some unpacked boxes, but he didn't appear to be among them. Walking into her own bedroom, she saw the kitten curled up on her bed. "You little stinker." She picked him up and stroked his fur. Thankfully, the search for him had calmed her nerves.

She re-entered the kitchen and saw David examining Becky's artwork on her refrigerator. "Becky's given you quite a lot of her artwork, I see."

"Yes. I don't know much about the capabilities of five-year-olds, but they seem quite good to me." Her breath came more naturally now, and she felt more able to converse with him calmly.

"Yeah. She's better than the other two were at her age."

Then he glanced towards the living room at the back of the house. "Can I look around a little? I haven't been in here since Mrs. Brower moved out. It looks different."

"Sure." She followed him into the living room. "I painted the walls to brighten it up a bit, and of course, the furniture's different. I didn't have to do much else; the house seems in great shape for its age."

David said he thought it could be close to a hundred years old, and that he'd always liked the old place. He wandered around the living room as he spoke, pausing at the stone fireplace. He told her that he liked the oriental rug that she'd gotten to cover the hardwood floor underneath the sofa and two chairs. "It looks nice," he said. "It's brighter, and yet you've kept the ambiance of the old place."

It had a quiet dignity and class just as she did, he thought.

"Thanks, I still have a few things that I want to do, of course . . . when I have more time."

He looked at his watch. "It's getting late. I'd better go."

Walking to the chair in which Smokey lay sleeping, he picked him up. Jessica walked with him to the door. But just before they reached it, he turned to her. "You . . . uh, wouldn't be interested in the San Francisco Symphony by any chance, would you?"

She wasn't sure what he meant. "I enjoy the symphony. Jim and I used to go occasionally. When we could afford it."

For a moment he seemed taken aback at her response. He paused for a moment, and after a look of puzzlement, proceeded. "A friend had tickets he couldn't use for tomorrow night and gave them to me. Would you care to go?"

"Uh . . . you mean. . . ." Was he was offering her the tickets or asking her to go with him?

He laughed at her befuddled expression. "I guess I'm not making myself clear. Would you care to go to the symphony with me tomorrow night?"

Her heart stopped and then it surged again with an excitement she couldn't control. He was asking her out on a date!

But then she clamped a lid on her swelling emotions. More probably, he had spare tickets and wanted to do her this favor in return for the few she'd done for Rachael and Becky. But either way, she shouldn't go. She'd vowed not to get any more involved.

"Jessica?"

"Uh . . . that sounds nice, David. I'd like to go." She flinched at the over-eager sound of her voice, but he didn't seem to notice. She was going for the music, she told herself. She hadn't been to the symphony in years.

"Good!" He sounded genuinely pleased. "It starts at eight o'clock. I'll pick you up at about six-thirty. The traffic into the city may be heavy at that time of night."

Jessica nodded, and told him she'd be ready.

His gaze met hers and then dropped to her lips. He resisted a sudden impulse to kiss her.

On the way home, a small voice kept telling him that he shouldn't have done it, shouldn't have arranged to spend a whole evening alone with her. He was attracted to her and sensed his feeling could become complicated. And he wasn't ready for a relationship. He had no time for one—he barely had time for the responsibilities he already carried. But she'd been so warm and responsive since the day he'd met her. Always so easy to talk to. He'd instinctively wanted to spend more time with her.

He could handle it, he told himself. Maybe they could just be friends.

At 7:20 the following evening, they drove the steep hills of San Francisco. As they came up over the top of one of them, San Francisco Bay, still dotted with a few of the afternoon's sailboats, came into view. Looking down at the Bay waters, they could see the

Oakland Bay Bridge and Alcatraz Island. The water seemed peaceful from this height, despite the reality of its treacherous currents.

San Francisco-style Victorian houses lined the streets down which they drove, and Jessica couldn't help thinking what a beautiful city it was. Tonight especially, it seemed a place of beauty and romance.

The symphony was wonderful. From their center seats, just a few rows from the front, they could see which instrument or combination of instruments produced each particular sound.

Jessica especially enjoyed watching the harpist as he produced his melodious strains. After one especially poignant passage, which she watched and listened to intently, she thought she felt David's gaze upon her. She turned to see a look of soft amusement in his eyes. Continuing to look deeply into them, trying to determine what the look meant, she smiled hesitantly. The next moment, she felt his hand cover hers as it lay on the chair arm between them. There was a possessiveness in his touch, and a thrill ran through her.

She tried to return her attention to the music, but his hand remained on hers, playing lightly with her fingers and creating a confusion in her mind. With the delicious sensation of his touch vying for her attention, the sound of the music seemed to fade into the background.

His hand still held hers as the music ended and the

lights came up for intermission. As the room brightened, she turned to look at him. He smiled again, still playing with her fingers. Heat spread through her. This time, she didn't try to resist it. His hazel eyes were flecked with gold and, as she watched, she saw an intensity grow within them. She felt his hand tighten around hers, and he pulled her toward himself. Slowly he bent his head to hers and touched her lips with his own. Then raising his head to look at her again, he brushed one finger of his free hand lightly over her cheek. "You're a delightful woman, Jessica. You have a refreshing sense of interest and wonder in everything around you. I enjoy being with you very much."

She swallowed hard. Instinctively, her free hand moved to his upper arm, and the rock-hard strength she felt there surprised her. She could sense the strength in his hand too, even as it held hers gently. "I enjoy being with you too, David," she said quietly, still looking into those intense hazel eyes.

His head bent towards her once more, and his lips touched hers. She found herself aching to be taken into his arms. For a moment she forgot where they were.

Then he straightened, seeming to grow aware of the movement of people around them. He grinned, sheepishly. "I guess this isn't the time nor the place."

She felt her face redden as she too looked around and saw several people with amused smiles, observing them.

"Shall we stretch our legs?" he asked. They moved into the lobby, still holding hands.

Chapter Four

The drive home was pleasant. Even though the evening had turned cool, they kept the windows partly open, breathing in the fresh air, already damp with the fog that rolled in most nights at this time of year. Jessica had grown to love the nighttime smell of the moisture-laden air. They could see the mounds of heavy clouds and fog in the dark sky, pushing inland over the hills between themselves and the ocean.

They discussed the symphony, and then David asked her about her career plans. She told him that she especially enjoyed her writing classes and that she envisioned a career in that area, probably technical writing to begin with since that was most likely to afford her a regular paycheck. And then who knows, she ventured, there were so many directions in which she could go. She told him that the possibilities excited her.

He turned strangely silent for some time after that.

When they reached her house, Jessica invited David in for a cup of tea, reluctant for the evening to end.

They took it into the living room. Jessie set the tray on the coffee table, and they both sat down on the sofa. After taking his first sip, David set his cup down and stared down into it. "Who's Jim, Jessica?" he asked in a subdued tone.

His question surprised her, and she found herself unable to answer for a moment.

"You mentioned him the other night." David continued. "Said you used to go to the symphony together."

A lump rose in her throat. "Jim was my husband."

His head came up. "Was?"

"Yes." Her voice dropped to a whisper. "He was killed in an automobile accident two years ago." The happiness she'd felt all evening drained away.

"I'm sorry, Jessica." He put his hand over hers. A pained look entered his face.

His hand felt somehow comforting and protective, and gave her the courage to continue. "We'd gone up to the mountains to ski for the weekend." Her voice took on a monotone quality, and she felt a small measure of the numbness she'd felt then. "We were on our way home on a Sunday night. It started snowing. Hard. The winding roads turned slippery." Her voice dropped to a whisper again. "It was a head-on colli-sion." Her throat closed; she choked and couldn't go on.

He moved to take her into his arms, cradling her head against his chest.

"Were you hurt?"

"My hip was broken and my left arm. But Jim . . . the impact was worse on his side of the car." She pressed her face against David's comforting bulk, see-ing the horror of it all again. She couldn't hold back the tears and cried quietly against him.

He held her and stroked her hair and whispered into it. "Jessie, I'm so sorry."

Somehow, his compassion helped. Eventually her sobs subsided.

She pulled away from him then, and standing, began to pace the room, stopping by the fireplace. Turning to look at him again, she immediately looked away, afraid his unmasked sympathy would make her cry again. "I'm sorry. I guess I still can't talk about it une-motionally." He stood too, but didn't approach her. She began to pace again. Saying nothing, remembering.

"Are you all right financially?"

She nodded. "Jim had investments." Her voice broke, and she took a deep breath. "I mean, I can get through school. And I have this house. But eventually I'll have to start earning a living."

He nodded without speaking.

She wiped the tears from her cheeks with the palms of her hand and smiled wanly. "I'm sorry, David. We've had such a nice time tonight, I didn't mean to spoil it.

"You haven't. Besides, I'm the one who asked."

"Would you like some more tea," she asked to change the subject, even though she could see that he'd hardly touched his.

"No, thanks." He watched her with concern.

She tried to smile again. "I'm all right, David. I haven't been this teary in a long time. It's just . . . thinking about it all again . . ." She shrugged.

"I know. I'm sorry I brought it up."

She walked to the window and looked out into the blackness for a long time, until he spoke again.

"Would you like me to leave?"

She turned to face him, wiping away tears that persisted in spilling over and swallowing the lump that threatened to rise again in her throat. "Maybe that would be best."

He eyed her with a worried expression. "I hate to leave you like this. Why don't you come and spend the night with us."

She shook her head and tried to smile, still not trusting herself to speak.

"Then let me sleep here on the couch. At least I'll be here if you need someone."

She took a deep breath and wiped both cheeks with the palms of her hands again, struggling to steady her voice. "I'm fine. Really. I guess I'd rather be alone right now."

"I don't think you should be alone, Jessica."

The lump eased from her throat and her voice became stronger. "It's been two years, David. I've learned to live with this. I promise you, I'll be all right."

He gave her a doubtful look, but after a few moments, moved towards the door. "I'll check with you tomorrow."

She nodded and pulled her mouth into something she hoped resembled a smile.

David paused at the door, took her by the shoulders and kissed her forehead. For some reason, it made her feel like crying again.

"You're sure you're okay?" he asked gruffly. When she nodded once more, he brushed her still damp cheek with his fingers again and backed out the door. He studied her once more with concern before shutting it behind himself.

At home, David paced his bedroom, thinking about Jessica. He'd taken every opportunity to come to know her, and his whole being had responded to what he'd learned. His feelings were rapidly developing into something more than platonic. Much more. They'd already grown into something he wasn't sure he could control.

He'd discovered that her outer beauty was also a reflection of her inner nature. She'd reacted with caring to any needs he and his family presented her. And yet, she had a quiet dignity and self-respect. She was capable of great love and devotion; he'd seen that in her attitude towards her husband.

David sighed deeply. But he had to put all of that out of his mind somehow, because he'd made his decision long ago. And that meant that he couldn't see her anymore. His first duty was to his children. He'd brought them into the world, and he was responsible for them. All of their futures might depend on his actions now.

Despite Jessica's wonderful qualities, she wanted a career. She'd spelled that out very clearly tonight. He'd heard the enthusiasm and excitement in her voice when she'd told him about her writing aspirations. And the last thing his family needed was to risk involvement with another career woman.

Perhaps putting the brakes on now was best thing for her too. She still seemed vulnerable. She'd lived through severe pain, and he didn't want to be the cause of any more for her. He couldn't let this continue any further.

He'd send Agatha over to check on her tomorrow. And perhaps he could keep himself appraised of her well-being through Pat. But, of one thing he was sure: He couldn't continue seeing her.

The events of that evening had given Jessica the impression that their friendship had taken on a new dimension, a new closeness. Therefore, she was surprised when she received visits from only Agatha and Becky over the next several days. She didn't see or hear from David at all that next week but consoled herself that he was probably busy with his work.

On Saturday morning, the telephone rang. It was Pat. "Jessica, help! We need someone to fill in for Brenda. Her baby is sick, and her husband is out of town."

"Give me fifteen minutes," Jessie told her. She was happy for the invitation and glad to hear from Pat again. It had been at least two weeks since they'd played tennis or talked, and Jessica had missed the camaraderie.

The other two women, who made up their doubles foursome, were pleasant, and their match proved enjoyable, despite the heat of the morning. Jessie guessed that the day would become a scorcher.

When they'd finished playing and the other women left, Pat suggested that she and Jessie get a cold drink at the club snack bar. They found a table by the window with a view of the tennis courts and settled down to enjoy their drinks. They'd been chatting for several minutes when they heard a cheerful voice behind them.

"Well, you ladies look like you're cooling off nicely." Jessica turned to see Brad approach their table with David close behind. David evidently didn't notice Jessica at first, but the minute recognition registered in his eyes, his smile faded.

"Mind if we join you?" Brad pulled out a chair. "We thought we'd get something cold before heading on home." Both men looked as though they'd had a hard game: Perspiration beaded their foreheads and wetted their shirts to their backs. Brad plopped down heavily. "Whew."

David remained standing, however, and shuffled his feet in obvious discomfort. "Uh . . . actually Brad, I think I'll pass. I've got a lot of work to do."

"But you're the one who suggested coming in here!"

David ignored the remark. "Nice to see you, Pat, Jessica," he nodded to each. "See you later, Brad." With a wave, he set off. The three at the table looked at each other with puzzled expressions.

Then slowly Brad shook his head. "That guy's going to push himself too hard some day. I worry about him."

Jessie felt stunned. How different David had acted from the last time they'd been together. Despite her reluctance, she realized that she had begun to count on his friendship. Upset and confused, she struggled to bring her attention back to the discussion at hand. "Does he bring work home over the weekend often?"

"Darn right. The minute the kids are in bed or away somewhere, he's back at it. Between the company and his family, he must work twenty hours a day. Of course, he'll never admit it. He doesn't count the hours he works at home."

Brad paused to give the waitress his drink order before continuing.

"He rarely takes any time for his own enjoyment. Tennis is his only self-indulgence."

"Then I guess it was unusual that he invited me to the symphony last Saturday night."

Her friends' mouths gaped. "You're kidding! Well, that's a first. I don't think he's had date since Cassandra left."

"You know, we thought he acted interested in you that day we all played mixed doubles," Pat injected.

"I wish." Jessica smiled ruefully, a little surprised herself at the admission. "But, I must have disillusioned him, because this is the first time I've seen him since last Saturday."

"Well, he *is* busy," Pat consoled, "not only with his kids but with his parents."

"His parents?" Jessica frowned. "I met his father at Rachael's graduation, but no one mentioned his mother."

"She's bedridden. Has Alzheimer's."

"Oh, how awful! Is she in a nursing home?"

"No. They keep her at home and have a nurse come in every day. David pays most of the bills. His parents don't have much money.

"His father was a teacher," Brad added. "And his mother's health has always been poor. Her medical bills ate up a large portion of their income. David probably would have had a tough time getting through college if he hadn't gotten a scholarship to Stanford. The poor guy's never had it easy for very long. Cassandra left just about the time the doctors diagnosed his mother's Alzheimer's. A lesser guy would have folded."

Jessica sat in silent thought. Everything she learned about David increased her respect and affection for him. But why had he acted so strangely today? She had watched his demeanor change the moment he saw her. She thought back to their last evening together; what had she done to cause his change in attitude? Suddenly, she became aware of movement around her.

"Ready to go, Jessie?" Pat and Brad had risen from the table. She followed them out of the restaurant.

On an afternoon of the following week, Becky appeared for one of her after-school visits, bringing Jessica another watercolor painting for the refrigerator exhibit. Jessie had studying to do, so she suggested that Becky draw more pictures with the paper and crayons that Jessica kept there for her.

Deeply involved in the assignment on which she was working, Jessica lost track of the time. She suddenly became aware that her doorbell had rung.

"I'll get it." Becky hopped up and ran to the door. "Hi, Daddy!"

Jessica dropped the book she'd been holding and looked up to see David enter.

Becky pulled him along by the hand. "I'm drawing some pictures for Jessica. Want to see?"

Jessie stood up slowly from her chair at the kitchen table. Sliding her hands into the back pockets of her jeans, she smiled at him tentatively.

He looked at her—but not into her eyes—and nodded. "Hello, Jessica." He didn't return her smile. His voice was polite but not particularly friendly.

Then he turned to Becky. "Sure, let's see them."

Jessica watched as he patiently listened to Becky's interpretation of her drawings. While the little girl continued to talk, David looked up, and his eyes met Jessica's. She knew that her own eyes questioned his behavior and was puzzled to see a resignation or a sadness in his. His attention returned to Becky as she finished her explanation.

Then he told her that Rachael and Tad had gone to a movie with friends and that Agatha had plans for the evening. "So I'm taking my girl out to dinner," he told her.

Becky brightened. "Can Jessica come too?"

Jessica stiffened, then squirmed. She saw the trapped look in David's eyes. "I've got a lot of work to do, Becky," she told the child, giving David an out.

"But you can work later," the little girl persisted. "It won't take long to eat dinner. Please, please, please?" She jumped up and down and clapped her hands.

"Becky!" David's firm voice interrupted her gaiety.

"Jessica said she has work to do. She can come with us some other time."

Jessica felt as though she'd been slapped. He didn't want her along and didn't make much attempt to hide it. She watched a deflated Becky put her crayons back in their box in silence.

David walked to the door and waited for his daughter, his hand on the doorknob and looking as though he couldn't wait to make his escape.

When the door closed behind them, Jessica swallowed irate tears until she heard the car pull away. Then they slid down her cheeks.

She felt confused, hurt, and angry. She was the one who had been reluctant to let their friendship progress beyond the casual stage. He had asked her out, had kissed her, and told her he enjoyed being with her. His kindness and apparent sincerity had almost made her forget her determination never to care for a man again.

The last time they'd been together, she had confided to him the most painful details of her life. He'd held her so tenderly, seemed to feel so intensely for her. Had all that been an insincere act? She couldn't believe it had. But then why was he behaving this way?

Out of necessity, Jessie spent most of the next few days either in class or at the school library. She had a term paper due and final exams were coming up.

Late one afternoon, after returning home, she decided to get some fresh air and, at the same time, complete a task that had been nagging at her.

She was in her front yard, pruning the unruly branches of several bushes that bordered the road, when she heard a car approach. Looking up, she saw David at the wheel of his gray sedan. She straightened and watched him, thinking he would surely stop or at least slow and say a few words. He waved, but continued on by, slowing only to turn into his own driveway.

Jessica watched him get out of the car. He gathered up his briefcase and what appeared to be several files and books, and then turned to walk toward the house without even glancing in her direction.

Indignation flared. "David!" She walked hurriedly toward him. He turned as she approached. Her determination wavered, but she forced herself to confront him. "Why are you acting this way, David? What have I done to offend you?"

"Nothing. Why?"

"Oh, come on. Your attitude towards me has completely changed since last Saturday night. I thought we had a pleasant time, that we were becoming friends."

He wouldn't let her hold his eye, looking from her face, to the car, to the ground. "You haven't done anything wrong," he mumbled.

"Then why are you acting so unfriendly?"

"Look, Jessica." He sounded exasperated. He squirmed, looking trapped. "I can't . . . I mean . . . I don't have time for personal relationships."

"You used to have time to at least be friendly."

Then he did look into her eyes, and what she saw stunned her: an empty hopelessness. And for the very briefest second, a tortured longing. "Please believe me, Jessica. This is the best I can do." His words seemed wrenched from his throat.

She stared at him, then nodded, and began to back away.

Suddenly Tad burst out the front door. "Dad, guess what! Oh, hi, Jessica!" He grinned a welcome at her. "Guess what, guys! I'm going to be on the swim team! Dad, will you show me how to do the butterfly?" He noticed the seriousness of their expressions and sobered. "What's the matter? Something wrong?"

Jessie spoke first. "No, nothing's wrong. Congratulations, Tad. The swim team should be fun." She could hear her voice quaver. Tad looked from her to his father, puzzled.

"Well, I've got to finish trimming my bushes before it gets dark." She waved with a hand that still hung at her side and continued backing away. Then she turned and headed for home.

Entering the house, David went directly to his study and closed the door. His encounter with Jessica had shaken him. In just a few moments, she'd awakened and sharpened in him again the needs that he'd been trying so long to ignore. She made him crave the warmth and softness of a woman again. Up until the

time he'd met her, he'd been able to handle the loneliness, but she was different.

And now his weakness and impulsiveness could end
up causing them both a great deal of grief. Why had
he even asked her to the darned symphony? He'd
known where his feelings were headed. But he had
been drawn to her and hadn't been able to stay away.

Well, he'd better learn to stay away. Before things
got any more complicated.

The next week, Jessica had to exert all her self-
discipline to concentrate on final exams. The first one
was in Medieval Literature, and as she scanned the
questions on the day of the exam, she realized that her
mind lacked sharpness and clarity.

After talking with David last week, she had had
several restless nights, and even last night, she had
slept poorly. Now she kept getting the cantos of
Dante's *Divine Comedy* mixed up. Had the adulterers
been in purgatory or hell? Both, she was pretty sure.
The difference had to have been in the degrees of the
perceived sins. With Paolo and Francesca, it seemed
to her, Dante showed the pain of their guilt, but also
the deep sweetness of their love. She hoped the professor would look kindly upon her answers.

She returned from taking the exam around dinner
time. As she unlocked her door, her telephone rang,
and she rushed to answer it.

"Hi, Jessie. This is Rachael. Will you send Becky home for dinner, please?"

"Becky?" Jessica frowned. "She isn't here. I haven't seen her today."

"But, Daddy . . ." Rachael sounded puzzled too. "Okay, thanks anyway.

Jessica replaced the receiver, then sat looking at it, perplexed. A vague uneasiness pricked at her. This wasn't the type of neighborhood where a small child might go any number of places. The houses were widely spaced, and Jessica could only think of one playmate that lived nearby. Her home was about a quarter of a mile away and on the other side of the road. A road which Becky wasn't allowed to cross by herself.

Then Jessica laughed at herself. She was being silly. Becky was probably somewhere at home. They most likely called before looking for her.

She walked to the couch, onto which she had tossed her books before answering the telephone and began flipping through her notes for clues about the accuracy of her answers.

The facts about the adulterers in Dante were pretty much on target. She hoped the instructor would like her reasoning. She went on to look up additional details on which she had based other answers and found that her recollection had been better than she'd expected. Maybe she hadn't done so poorly after all.

She jumped as the phone rang again. This time it was David.

"Jessica, have you seen Becky at all this afternoon?"

"No, David, I haven't. Haven't you found her yet?"

"She's nowhere in the house or yard. Agatha's sick so I came home this afternoon. I was working in my office when Becky came home from school. She said she was going over to your house. I never gave it a second thought." He paused for a moment and his next words seem to hold a hint of panic. "God, where could she be? It's been hours."

"I've been gone all day. Maybe she's been here. I'll go and look around outside."

"Yeah, all right. Let me know."

Chapter Five

Jessica scoured both the front and back yards, looking anywhere a child might hide. She walked out to the road and looked both ways. She even walked to a nearby bend in the road, but Becky was nowhere in sight.

Hurrying toward the Bennington house, she searched every imaginable hiding place along the way to no avail. She hoped and prayed that Becky would somehow be safely at home when she got there.

She walked into the house without knocking.

Rachael came from the direction of the kitchen with a hopeful look in her eyes, which immediately faded and turned troubled. "Daddy's on the telephone calling people, but so far no one's seen her." Jessie knew that Rachael had hoped it had been Becky who'd entered.

David came out of the kitchen with the same expectant look. Tad followed. When David saw her, his eyes turned questioning.

She shook her head. "I couldn't find her anywhere. Have you checked the woods?"

David nodded. "There's a board out of the fence back there. I'm going to climb over and have a look." The Bennington property extended for about fifty feet back of the house, the farthest point of which was wooded and fenced. "Tad, you come with me. Rachael, you keep calling . . . anyone you can think of."

"Shall I drive around the neighborhood? Maybe she wandered up the road?"

"I was going to do that next, but yeah, thanks, Jessica." He tossed her the keys to his car. She saw the worry on his face, but he seemed in control.

Jessie drove for several blocks in either direction. Then she took a few of the side roads, but Becky was nowhere in sight. She returned to the house.

"They're still not back," Rachael told her in a shaky voice. "And I can't think of anybody else to call. No one's seen her."

Jessie gave her a reassuring hug. "We'll find her." She hoped she sounded more confident than she felt.

Then she walked to the back door and stepped outside. Hearing voices coming from the wooded area, she headed toward them. She had covered about half the distance to the trees when David and Tad appeared, walking toward her. Both looked alarmed. David held up something which she couldn't quite discern.

As he neared, she could make out a piece of cloth— the same pattern as the knit top Becky had worn the first day Jessica met her. "She's been back there." David told her. "This was snagged on the fence. God only knows how far she's wandered. There are ditches and snakes back there. "I'm going to call the police." He brushed by Jessica and headed for the house.

She turned to follow him, running to keep up. "Smokey. Is he here?"

David shook his head. "He's gone too."

When they got to the house, David went immediately to the telephone and called the police. After he'd finished, he turned back to them looking distracted. "They're coming." He paced the floor in silence. No one spoke until the doorbell rang several minutes later.

The policemen, two of them, appeared calm. They asked for a physical description of Becky. When had the family last seen her? Was there anywhere she'd be likely to go by herself?

David explained the circumstances of her disappearance and told them that Jessie's was the only place she'd go alone. He added that they'd checked with all the neighbors and any friends they could think of, but no one had seen her.

David showed them the piece of cloth and then took them to where he'd found it. They were gone a long while.

When they returned, it was getting dark. The policemen were still asking questions, but of a different nature. Was Becky likely to befriend strangers? Had anyone seen any strange or suspicious persons lurking around lately? Jessica saw the fear in David's eyes turn to sheer panic. Almost immediately, however, a curtain of control descended over his features. He explained that she was a friendly child but had been told repeatedly, both at home and in school, not to talk to strangers.

Jessie couldn't help remembering the afternoon Becky had come over to talk to her, a stranger then, while searching for Smokey.

"David, maybe they should know about Smokey."

"Smokey, ma'am?"

"Yes. Smokey's her kitten." Jessica explained that twice before, the kitten had run away, and at least one of those times, Becky had gone looking for him. Smokey was missing now.

Just then the doorbell rang. Pat and Brad entered with another neighbor. When David told them that Becky was still missing, they offered to help in a search for her. They told David that other neighbors were outside, too, offering to help.

Suddenly a commotion from the front yard interrupted them, and they turned to see a car pull into the Bennington driveway. Through the window they saw the car stop and an elderly man get out. He bent back into the car as if to reach for something, and when he straightened again, he held a small child.

David raced out the door.

Still watching from the window, Jessie saw him take the child from the elderly man. It was Becky.

Jessica felt weak with relief.

Seconds later David strode back into the house, carrying the disheveled child. The elderly man followed.

Becky had a dirty, tear-stained face, and clutched her gray kitten. One side of her little knit shirt had a large tear.

Rachael and Tad ran forward to greet her with relieved exclamations. As they did, the kitten jumped out of Becky's arms, apparently frightened by the excitement.

A surge of alarm rose in Becky's eyes, and they flashed to the open door. Her arms reached out in an effort to retrieve the kitten. "The door! Close the door! He'll get out!" she screamed.

"It's all right, Becky. We've closed the door." David soothed.

Then her dirty little face dissolved into tears. "Daddy, I left the door open again, and he got out. I tried to find him."

"Oh, Becky, Becky." He hugged her small body to himself and buried his face in her shoulder, his eyes closed. She wrapped her arms around his neck, crying softly. He held her quietly for some time, and Jessica felt her throat tighten with emotion.

A moment later, David had composed himself. He turned to thank the elderly gentleman for bringing Becky home.

The man said that Becky told him her cat had gotten out of the house and then slipped through a hole in the fence. She'd followed him down the strip of county land that ran back of the properties here.

The cat had strayed into his yard first, and he'd taken him inside. A short while later, he'd heard Becky, crying and calling.

He'd driven her around, trying to find where she lived. She'd wandered almost half a mile, but recognized the neighborhood as they'd approached. Then he'd seen the commotion outside the house.

When everyone had gone, and Rachael had pried Becky from David's arms to bathe her, Jessica sat with David and Tad. "How could I have been so careless?" David chastised himself.

"She said she was coming to my house. How could you have known?" Jessica comforted gently.

"That fence should have been kept in repair. If the board hadn't fallen out, even if the cat had gotten away, at least Becky couldn't have followed. It's rough terrain back there."

"We were just back there last week, Dad. It wasn't out then."

"David," Jessie consoled logically. "We all try our

best, but things don't always work out perfectly. You're carrying a heavy load here."

He looked up at her and gave her a weak smile. "Thanks, Jess . . . it helps." He studied her. "You help . . . whenever any of us need you."

Then he turned and slapped his son lightly on the knee. "And thank you too, sport. Now, you'd better get off to bed. You have swimming practice early tomorrow morning."

"All right, Dad. But first I'll walk Jessica home."

David looked towards the hallway where the voices of the girls echoed from the bathroom. Jessica could see that he didn't want to leave Becky yet—that he needed to assure himself again that she was really all right."

Acting like the responsible young man he was becoming, Tad walked Jessica to her front door. She gave him a hug before he left, and for just a second, he seemed to cling to her.

When she got into bed that night, Jessica couldn't fall asleep. Her emotions had been in such a turmoil all evening that she just couldn't unwind. She threw back the covers and padded out to the kitchen in her pajamas, deciding to see if hot milk would help to make her sleepy.

The white liquid had just started bubbling around the edges of the pan when she heard a light knock at her door. She looked at the clock: 1 A.M. Who would be knocking at this time of night? She walked to the door and stood listening. When she heard nothing, she called out. "Who is it?"

"It's David, Jessie." His low voice sounded husky.

She opened the door, and he stood looking down at her. A light breeze ruffled his hair. He wore jeans and a soft leather jacket. "I was out walking and saw your light on. I guessed that you couldn't sleep either."

She stepped aside to allow him to enter. "You guessed right. I was just making myself some hot milk, would you like some?" He made a face, and she couldn't help laughing. "My mother says it works."

He smiled. And it seemed good to see that smile again. She realized that it had been quite some time since she'd last seen it. For the past two weeks, he'd been so somber and abrupt. And then, of course, tonight he'd been worried about Becky.

"Okay. Guess I'll try anything." He tossed his jacket onto a kitchen chair and came to stand near her at the stove.

She turned the milk off and reached up to get another cup out of the cupboard. As she filled the cups, she could feel his presence close behind her, and then she caught the familiar scent of his after-shave. The heat that suddenly flooded her shook her composure, and she quickly set the pan down as her hand began to shake. To calm her trembling, she reminded herself of the way he'd rebuffed her the past weeks, only welcoming her tonight when he needed her help and emotional support. Even now, he most likely just needed to talk . . . to someone . . . anyone.

Then she felt his hands on her shoulders, turning her to himself. Looking into her eyes, he slowly slid his hands up to cup her face. He drew her mouth towards his, and she could feel herself tremble as their lips touched.

Then David pulled back to look into her face again, as if seeking permission. She knew that her eyes begged for more, despite the nagging at the back of her mind that asked why. Why now, after weeks of rebuffs? But she was powerless to pull away.

Again his lips descended to touch hers softly. This time she couldn't help returning his kiss.

She could feel the effect go through him like an electric shock. His body stiffened and shuddered. Suddenly, he was deepening their kiss with an almost desperate intensity. Emitting a low groan, he drew her into his arms. She felt the demanding strength in them, and their heat seemed to sear her body where he held her. She felt herself go limp.

Then his face was in her hair and words seemed wrenched from his throat in an agony of feeling. "Oh God, Jessie, Jessie. I need you. I've needed you for so long."

Need, her brain screamed. Need. Nothing more.

Nevertheless, her breath came in jerky gasps as his hands caressed her back. His scent filled the fog of emotion that enveloped her mind. Then his mouth found hers again, and she clung to him.

"I need you, Jessie," he groaned again when next he broke their kiss.

But in the voice of memory, somewhere in the haze of her mind, she heard those other words, always before associated with these searing emotions: *I love you, Jessie.*

Oh God! Jim! Suddenly cold reality was upon her. With a desperation she tore herself from his arms. She stumbled into the living room, trying to put as much distance as possible between them. Blindly her hands encountered the cold stone of the fireplace. Grasping the mantel with white knuckles, she fought to bring her breathing under control. When the heaving in her chest began to subside, she pressed her forehead to the cool mantel. A long time seemed to pass before she heard a movement behind her.

"I'm sorry, Jessica." His voice sounded hoarse and strained.

She nodded.

Long minutes passed again, and she heard the back door open. After another moment she turned to look. The door stood ajar, and David was nowhere in sight.

Shakily she walked to the open doorway. He sat outside on one of the patio chairs, elbows on his knees and head in his hands. She stepped outside, hugging herself.

He must have heard her, but he didn't move.

She spoke softly. "I'm sorry too, David. I know you needed someone tonight."

He shook his head. "You deserve so much better than that, Jessica. I had no right to kiss you. I can't get involved." And then after a pause. "It's just that I can't seem to get you out of my mind. And then tonight when Becky disappeared . . . the fear, the desperation. And you were there. You're always there when I need you. And I'm finding I need you more and more." He spoke the last statement in a whisper.

She stood looking down at him and a myriad of emotions shook her. A foolish joy at his admitted attachment to her. Reluctant agreement that they couldn't get involved.

Because she could never forget Jim—the joy of having him and the pain of losing him. And she could never forget the panic and vulnerability at being left alone, with limited resources and unable to support herself. She had to come to terms with all of these issues. She didn't have the time or the emotional energy for a romantic entanglement. Besides, David's idea of romance apparently revolved around his own *needs*, not caring.

He spoke, interrupting her thoughts. "Was my kiss really that distasteful, Jessica?" At her questioning look, he added, "You couldn't seem to get away from me fast enough."

She sat down in the chair facing him, her knees still shaking. "It's just that . . . my husband, Jim . . . is the only other person who has held me that way. Suddenly all I could think of was him and the relationship we had." She held David's gaze with her own. "Only where you kept using the word *need*, he always said *love*."

David felt a wave of self-disgust. He'd acted like a selfish jerk tonight. He *had* thought only of his own needs—if he'd thought at all. Jessica had troubles of her own. He remembered her anguish the night of the symphony, when she'd told him about her husband's death. He closed his eyes and covered his face with his hands. "I'm sorry, Jessica."

"I know you needed someone tonight," she repeated. "But I also know you didn't necessarily need me."

He pulled his hands from his face and, looking at her, shook his head. "You're wrong. It's you I needed." His eyes burned into hers.

She looked away, afraid she might move towards him again. She had to keep her mind clear. And she had to—for some reason she couldn't explain—clarify their relationship. Staring down at her hands, which grasped one crossed knee, she paused to gather her thoughts. Then her eyes met his again.

"I'm confused by your reactions to me, David. For a while I thought we were growing closer. Becoming friends." *Could they be just friends*? She pushed the intrusive thought away. "I enjoyed our evening at the symphony. I thought you did too. But since that night you've treated me with indifference, almost disdain. I don't think I deserve that."

He seemed shocked at her description of his behavior. "It was far from disdain, Jessica." His gaze flickered away for a moment but then came back to hers. "I'm sorry for the way I've acted lately. You see, my feelings for you are becoming much more than I can afford to let them become. I find myself needing to be with you. I can't let that happen." He looked out into the night and then back at her. "We want different things from life. Any involvement between us would only lead to unhappiness."

She remained silent, needing to hear all of his reasoning.

"You want a career. I saw the night we went out together that you're very adamant and enthusiastic about that."

Her back straightened in mild defensiveness. "I need to know that I can take care of myself. You don't know what it's like to one day find yourself alone and without the education and skills to earn a reasonable living."

"Maybe not. But I know what it's like to have study and work come first to the woman in my life. What it's like to watch my children in pain because of it. To watch Rachael turn shy and unsure of herself because she thinks she's not worthy of her mother's time and attention. Watch Tad turn bitter because no matter how hard he tries at his studies or athletic endeavors, nothing captures his mother's interest or enthusiasm. Cassandra's studies and the law have come before anyone in the family since the day she went back to school."

His eyes met hers. "That's why I don't think it's a good idea to let anything get started between us. Our aims and desires are too much at odds. I'm drawn to you, and if we keep seeing each other, I'd become tempted to ignore our incompatibility." He smiled wanly. "As you've seen, I've already let that happen a time or two."

Jessica lowered her gaze, trying to ignore the sensation that something precious was in the process of slipping away. Despite all of the arguments to the contrary, something inside of her wanted to hold on. To try to find some solution to their dilemma. But she only nodded sadly. "All things considered, I guess I agree."

"Life is finally going smoothly for my family now. We've got Agatha, and we're reasonably happy—except for occasional episodes with Cassandra. I can't allow a relationship of my own to threaten that stability. I promised myself long ago never to create another situation that could disrupt my children's lives."

"I understand. And I agree, David."

He rose. "I'd better go." He started to walk away, then stopped. "Thank you for all you did tonight. I wish things could be different between us. If I've upset you, please forgive me."

She nodded, and again experienced the sensation that something precious was slipping away. She remembered all that Pat and Brad had told her about David: of the terrible burdens he bore. The realization of the kind of man he was engendered a regret that she could never be a part of his life. But he was right. They wanted and needed different things.

David turned and headed for home, and Jessica watched until he had disappeared into the blackness of the night.

She relived the scene between them a hundred times. Only the necessity of studying for the remainder of her final exams and completing the final draft of her Technical Writing term paper enabled her to finally put David out of her mind. She willed herself to concentrate on her work, telling herself that her livelihood depended on the results of her efforts.

She had a final meeting with her technical writing team. Their design for the computer classroom looked good. They assembled all their graphics and inserted them in their appropriate places. Especially impressive were the classroom layout designs she'd gotten from the instructor at Stanford and pictures and descriptions of the new style of recessed-top computer table, which Chris, one of the young men on her team, had obtained. Their report totaled 66 pages. Chris would rush it to the printer immediately so that it would be ready by the deadline date.

She reviewed all complex punctuation rules and sentence constructions and went over copy-editing symbols for her technical editing class. She assembled her *Chicago Manual of Style* and other reference books that students would be allowed to take into the classroom for the exam.

She skimmed and reread many of the Shakespeare plays they'd covered in her literature class, knowing that she would have to identify excerpts. She memorized passages—the instructor had said he'd ask them to write several from memory—selecting some of the most well-known ones in the hope that their vague familiarity over the years would help to prompt her memory. Such as Polonius' parting words to his son, Laertes, in Hamlet:

> This above all: to thine own self be true,
> And it must follow, as the night the day,
> Thou canst not then be false to any man.

She paused in her rereading of the passage. Were there words of wisdom here for her too?

Finally, when she'd finished her exams and handed in the completed term paper, Jessica felt drained. She almost wished she hadn't enrolled in the two summer classes. However, by doing so and also taking an extra class in the fall, she thought she could graduate by December. She reminded herself of the importance of getting her degree as soon as possible. Her money wouldn't last forever.

She had promised her parents that she would come home to Colesville for a visit between final exams and the beginning of summer classes, and she was looking forward to the rest and relaxation. She needed to get away for a while. She would have over a week to spend with them.

As she drove towards her hometown, she felt the tension and worry drain away. She smiled with pleasure as she saw the open fields and the soft rolling hills.

When she arrived, her parents greeted her with smiles and a warm welcome. Her mother had made her favorite chicken and dumpling dish and a fresh strawberry pie for her first dinner at home. Jessica bathed in the warmth, love, and relaxation.

Lying in her childhood bed that first night, she began to wonder why she had specialized in studies that would require her to work in Silicon Valley. She could easily switch her English major from the Career Writing emphasis to that of Literature. She could then get a teaching credential and teach here at the quiet little elementary school. She knew she always had a home with her parents. It was so peaceful and safe here.

And her emotions were safer here too. Back in the Bay Area, her attraction to David had all but destroyed her determination to avoid any romantic entanglement—only to encounter a similar determination in him. Why should she make her own life so difficult when it could instead be so easy?

Jessica spent long afternoons in the hammock under the large cherry tree in the backyard. Sometimes she read, and at other times, lying on her back, she looked and watched the birds and squirrels nibble at the dark red fruit. She helped her mother can cherries and make cherry pies. She even worked a few afternoons in the family bookstore.

One afternoon, Jessica and an old high-school friend drove up to the Lake Tahoe area to hike. They took Jessica's favorite trail to Fallen Leaf Lake. The exertion of climbing and the solitude of the tree-studded hills were a soothing balm to her mind and soul.

But as her week's visit drew to a close, she found herself becoming restless. Colesville and her parents' home had once again been a place of refuge and healing, as it had been after Jim's death. But now she realized it was time to go back into the world again. To stand on her own two feet. And as she drifted off to sleep the last night of her visit, her thoughts returned to the memory of David's embrace, and ironically, she experienced an emotion akin to homesickness.

Chapter Six

The following evening, a Sunday, found her driving back to the San Francisco Bay Area. The closer she got, the heavier the freeway traffic became. As she approached the Bay Area from the slightly elevated roadway, the vast stretch of buildings and concrete made her momentarily long to be back in the country.

But then she switched freeways and headed more directly towards Woodsborough, and the scenery changed. The traffic became lighter. Buildings became sparser and soon tree-covered hills appeared.

After exiting the freeway, the road she followed became winding. In several areas, trees encroached upon the road, their branches sometimes covering it, tunnel-like. The green hills were rapidly changing to summer brown, but they were open and airy.

Smiling, Jessica understood why she'd been attracted to this area. It was a quiet oasis, much like her perception of her childhood home but near the necessary hubbub of the business world. Surprisingly, she found it evoked in her those warm feelings associated with home. She became eager for the sight of her little house. When she thought of facing David again, she felt stronger, more self-confident.

She stayed at school until late afternoon that first day of summer classes and arrived home feeling fatigued. They weren't starting out slowly as regular quarter-length classes did. The professors had jumped right into the bulk of the workload, apparently because the courses were condensed into half the usual twelve-week period. She could see that she was going to have her hands full with two of them this summer.

As she pulled into her driveway, she noticed Becky at her front door. The child waved and then stood watching as Jessica got out of the car. "You were gone a long time. Pat said you'd be home yesterday." Jessica had asked Pat to pick up her mail while she was gone.

"Well, I did get home yesterday, but kind of late."

Becky ran to her and gave her a warm hug. In addition to her week's absence, Jessica hadn't seen Becky or any of the Benningtons during finals week. She had missed them. She returned Becky's hug with feeling.

Then Jessie heard another voice. "Jessica!" Rachael came walking towards them. "I thought I'd find Becky here. She kept coming over yesterday, looking for you, and she's been here twice today. I didn't think you were home yet."

Then yet another voice rang out. "Jessie!" Tad hung out the window of the family wagon, waving as he and Agatha drove by and turned into the Bennington driveway.

"Agatha picked Tad up from swimming practice," Rachael explained.

Tad got out of the car and ran towards Jessie and the girls. "You missed my first swim meet. I won first place in the breast stroke."

"That's great, Tad."

"Maybe you could come to our next home meet. It's in two weeks at our club."

"Sure, I'll come if I can."

"Welcome back, Jessie." Agatha had followed close behind Tad.

"Thank you, Agatha. I feel very properly welcomed home. Why don't you all come in. I brought back some of my mother's home-made chocolate chip cookies, and I have some milk in a grocery bag in the car." They all trooped inside.

An hour later, they sat around the kitchen table with empty milk glasses and crumb-littered plates in front of them when a knock sounded at the kitchen door. Answering it, Jessica found herself face to face with

David. He smiled down at her and looked into her eyes. "Hello, Jessie."

Uh oh! She wasn't going to fall into that trap again. She looked away from him and back at the table. "Come in. Your whole family's here." She tried to sound casual.

He followed her inside. God, he'd missed her. He'd felt so empty without her, especially since he knew that he'd have to remain without her. And now his whole being reveled in her presence. She looked great, as always. He felt his response to her slipping out of control once again.

Then his eyes took in his family. Apparently they'd missed her almost as much as he had. They were all growing closer to her every day, and it worried him more than a little. He supposed he should do something about it, but he sure as heck didn't know what. Forbid them to come over here? How could he do that? Did his insistence on staying away from her make him the only foolish one in the group?

He pushed the question from his mind and tried to sound casual. "I wondered where everyone'd gone. What's going on?"

"Jessica brought back cookies," Becky told him. "We're having some."

"Would you care for one?" Jessica was pleased with the polite but detached tone of her own voice.

"Sure." He joined them at the table, and Tad

launched into an immediate narration about swim practice.

As they all listened, Jessica couldn't keep her gaze from David. He looked more handsome than ever. Her heart did a little flip when he ran his fingers through his hair and then tugged at his tie to loosen it. Then as if he felt her watching him, he looked up, and his gaze held hers with its intensity. She couldn't look away and experienced that dangerous melting sensation that any contact with him seemed to evoke in her. Even now. Even after they'd both decided they were incompatible.

Then, as if from far away, she realized that Agatha had addressed her. She really must get home and start dinner, she said. Would Jessica care to join them to celebrate her homecoming?

"No . . . no thank you," Jessie stammered. "I've got a lot of preparation to do for my classes tomorrow."

Clucking like a mother hen, Agatha ushered the children out the door.

David exited last and paused to look into Jessica's eyes once more, chastising himself even as he did it. "It's good to see you again, Jessie. It seemed that you were gone a long time."

She nodded. "It seemed that way to me too."

He reached for her and she took a step backward. "Please don't, David. We've settled our relationship, let's not confuse things again."

He looked at her for a moment and then nodded

sadly. "You're right." He paused and tried to smile. "Welcome home."

David walked towards home slowly. He had to make himself stay away. But he guessed there was no reason his kids had to do so. They could be friends with her even if he couldn't. They'd been fond of Mrs. Brower when she lived here and visited often. No harm had come from that.

Yes, his relationship with Jessica was a nonissue as far as the children were concerned. As long as he stayed away from her, things would remain uncomplicated. But as he plodded away from Jessica's little cottage, he realized that he was performing the least difficult part of what would be demanded of him in the future. Keeping his thoughts from her would be a more difficult task.

Jessica entered the house the next afternoon and fell onto the couch. Her workload for just these two classes was becoming unbelievably heavy. In addition, thoughts of David had disturbed her concentration all day. She had steadfastly resisted them with mixed results. She had to be firmer with herself. David had his agenda and she had hers. And her livelihood might literally depend on her being able to put and keep him out of her mind. So she'd better start doing so right this minute, she told herself, if she hoped to accomplish any studying this evening.

Then she noticed the blinking of her answering machine. She pulled herself off the sofa and walked over to push the button. "Hello, Jessica. It's Pat. Brad and I are having a tenth wedding anniversary party this Saturday, and we hope you can come. Call me, okay?"

She dialed Pat's number. "Hi, Jessie. Can you come? It starts at five until whenever."

Of course, Jessica told her she'd come. Pat was becoming a good friend, and she didn't want to miss their celebration.

"Sorry to invite you so late, but you were away. We're going to barbecue, and then afterward Brad's brother and a couple of friends are going to play music. They're bringing a keyboard and a couple of guitars, and we may even have some dancing."

Jessica told Pat that it sounded like fun and that she was looking forward to it.

With her hectic schedule, the week flew by, and before Jessie knew it, Saturday had arrived. She studied until the last possible moment and beyond, then bathed and dressed, realizing she would arrive at least half an hour late at the party.

She wore the white sleeveless sun dress she'd bought just that week especially for today. The style flattered her figure and the color accentuated her subtle hint of a tan. She realized that, as much as she had tried not to, she'd selected the dress hoping that David would like it.

Something fluttered in her stomach as she rang Brad and Pat's doorbell. She would know very few people at this party and hoped that at least some of Pat's tennis friends would be here. They were always friendly.

A pleasant-looking man answered the door. "Hello. Come on in." He had an open and friendly expression. "Pat and Brad are around here somewhere." As she entered the house, he extended his hand to her. "I'm Jeff Gordon, an old college roommate of Brad's."

Jessica introduced herself, explaining that she lived across the street.

He seemed immediately interested and asked if she lived in the old house. When she answered in the affirmative, his eyes lit up. "I know quite a bit about its history." He spoke with sincere enthusiasm. Before they could discus the subject, however, Pat came towards them.

"I see you've met Jeff."

Jessica explained that he'd just introduced himself. "He was about to tell me something about the history of my house."

"I'll bet. Jeff's a professor of history at Stanford. He's interested in anything old."

"If I remember correctly, the original owners of your house owned a large portion of the land that's now Woodsborough," Jeff continued. "They parceled it off and sold it too early to make any big money, of course." He offered to look up more of the details for her if she were interested.

Jessica said that she would appreciate any information he could find.

Just then two of the women with whom Pat and Jessica had played tennis joined them. After chatting for a few moments about their last game, they suggested playing another and settled on a date and time.

As the women talked, Jessica's gaze scanned the room. She didn't see David anywhere. If he didn't come it was probably for the best. They didn't seem able to carry on a lucid conversation lately without straying into forbidden territory.

Just then, Brad popped his head in from the patio and announced that the barbecued steaks would be ready in ten minutes.

Pat scurried off to take the other dishes out of the refrigerator, as Jessica joined the mass exit towards the patio.

When they'd all seated themselves at the tables outside, Jessica found herself next to Jeff. He talked during most of the meal about the history of the Bay Area and especially of Silicon Valley.

She only vaguely heard the names of some of the early entrepreneurs: Bill Hewlett, David Packard, Robert Noyce. Normally she'd have been very interested but for some reason her mind kept returning to the question of why David hadn't come tonight. These were his best friends. How could he miss their party?

She struggled to bring her attention back to Jeff's monologue, realizing she'd missed a lot. In his recitation of the history of Silicon Valley, he had already arrived at the 60's and 70's, and his sentences were sprinkled with mention of semiconductors and integrated circuits.

Soon everyone had finished eating and had begun to circulate again. Then Brad's brother and a woman, both with guitars, and another man with a keyboard began playing a soft melody.

A few people began dancing on the patio, and Jeff turned to Jessica.

"Would you care to dance?"

It was the last thing she felt like doing, but she agreed. Jeff seemed like such a pleasant young man, but during their mealtime conversation, she'd seen his gaze dart repeatedly toward another young female guest. Jessica wondered why he didn't ask her to dance.

They had been moving around the dance floor only a short time when Jessica absently saw the door to the house open and David's form suddenly filled the doorway.

To her annoyance, her heart began to pound, and she felt the power of his magnetism. It seemed that if Jeff weren't holding her, she would be physically drawn to David. Why couldn't she stop reacting to him this way?

Suddenly she realized that David was looking at her too, and that Jeff had released her. The music had stopped. She couldn't pull her eyes from David's, and he closed the short distance between them.

"Hello, Jessica." He spoke tentatively, as though he weren't sure what kind of reception he'd receive.

"Hello, David. I thought maybe you weren't coming."

He paused for a moment, studying her, and she cringed, wondering if he'd caught the obvious implication that she had thought about him and looked for him.

"I just got back from L.A. an hour ago." His eyes held hers.

"Business?"

"Yeah." Then he looked at the tables being cleared. "Looks like I missed the food." He nodded to Jeff. They obviously knew each other.

Then Pat joined them. "Are you hungry, David? Come on, we'll find you something to eat." She pulled him towards the kitchen. His eyes continued to hold Jessica's until Pat had turned him away. Jessica noticed that several female guests' gazes followed them into the house.

Jeff questioned Jessica about her work, and then finding that she was a student, about her studies. Then he again asked her to dance. She reluctantly allowed herself to be led back to the dance floor.

The musical number had just entered its last few bars when she noticed David return to the yard. Jessica's heart leaped when she saw that his gaze immediately sought her out. But then, to her confusion, his eyes turned icy, and he continued watching her coldly until the music stopped. Another man approached David just then and seemed to engross him in conversation.

And as the music ended and they stopped dancing, a young man began talking to Jeff also. Standing idly by, Jessica's eyes drifted back to David. His gaze flickered towards her once and seemed to harden. Then an attractive young woman approached him, slipping her arm through his. Jessica watched David's eyes warm as they settled on the woman, and in a few moments they were laughing and chatting together. And *flirting* in Jessica's estimation!

She refused to watch this! She looked around for someone to talk to, but everyone she knew seemed engrossed in a conversation of their own. Jessica stood, idle and alone, for several minutes. Then seeing Pat come out of the house, she made a decision and moved quickly.

"Pat, I'm sorry, but I have to leave. I have so much work to do before Monday with these accelerated summer classes. I hope you understand.

Pat frowned at her. "Are you all right? You seem upset?"

"No, no, I'm fine, just very busy."

She bid Pat good-bye and had made her way half way down the driveway when a voice called out behind her.

"Jessica!"

She knew that voice and turned to see a broad form approach in the near darkness. As he drew closer, she could see that his eyes reflected a stern intensity. "What's going on, Jessica?"

"I'm going home." Without knowing why, she felt on the verge of tears.

"I mean what's going on between you and Jeff."

"Jeff?" She frowned in puzzlement. "Nothing's going on. We were just dancing."

"Dancing pretty closely, it seemed to me."

"Don't you think that's kind of a presumptuous accusation under the circumstances? Besides, you and that . . . woman . . . seemed to be having a pretty cozy conversation."

He looked confused for a moment and then the anger returned. "Don't be ridiculous. And don't try to change the subject."

"Why should it matter to you whether there's anything going on between Jeff and myself?"

He studied her for several moments. "I guess it shouldn't." He reached for her, however, and cupped her face with his hands. "But it does matter, Jessica. God help me, it does." His face reflected strong emotion.

Then for just a moment, his aspect brightened a bit. "I don't know, Jessie, maybe there's some way we could. . . ." But he didn't finish and in the next moment, the light faded from his eyes.

David shook his head. The similarities between Jessica and Cassandra raced through his mind. Both had married young. Both had gone back to school. Both were excited about careers. They were Cassie's children, and she didn't stay. How could he realistically expect more of Jessica? No, he thought, I can't gamble my children's futures.

"Maybe somehow what?"

He shook his head. "Nothing."

"Good night, David." But for a long moment, she didn't turn away.

"I'll watch until you get inside."

She turned and walked towards home.

David couldn't bring himself to go back to the party. He had known that someday he might have to face Jessica's relationship with another man, but he hadn't bargained for this: Nothing had prepared him for the way it tore at his gut tonight to see another man holding her.

His memory registered the picture of Jeff and Jessica dancing together once again. And suddenly the reality of what he had seen and the memory of Jessie's puzzlement at his accusation evoked a bitter, self-deprecating laugh. Good grief, they hadn't been dancing particularly close. He'd overreacted to an innocent situation. And Jeff was such a shy, serious guy, so consumed with things of the past. David couldn't think of anyone with whom Jessica's virtue would be safer.

But then his relief subsided and his stomach knotted

again. Someday he'd have to face her relationship with another man, and if his reaction to an innocent dance was any indication, he was in for some hellish times. David began walking dejectedly towards home.

And she was right. He'd been presumptuous in questioning her under the circumstances—in trying to hold her to an impossible situation. He knew it was the result of a struggle between his reason telling him what he should do, and his glands telling him what he wanted.

He stopped in the middle of his driveway and looked up at the sky, for some reason remembering the night they'd looked up at the same stars together. David shook his head. No, Jessie was more than glands. She was kindness and softness, and unadulterated class—along with those feminine curves that drove him crazy when he saw them by day and when they entered his dreams at night. And since the physical encounter with her the night of Becky's disappearance, he had become even more obsessed with her than before.

But he'd never know what it was like to possess her. The thought caused the familiar hopelessness to suffuse his being.

God, he was tired. He walked up the steps and entered the quiet house, longing for the sweet anesthesia of sleep.

Chapter Seven

Late the following week, Jessica walked into the house and threw her books down on the living room sofa in frustration. What was wrong with her? Her churning emotions over David were making it difficult for her to concentrate on her schoolwork. Why couldn't she forget him? He didn't want her!

She had fallen behind terribly this week, and she couldn't afford to do that. Just keeping up was difficult enough without having to catch up too. All week long she'd had trouble focusing both in class and with her reading assignments. She berated herself for her lack of self-discipline.

Then she heard a light knock at the door. Opening it, she beheld a radiant Becky, all dressed up and smiling proudly. "I came to show you the new dress my mother bought me." Stepping into the house, she did a little pirouette for Jessica's benefit.

"It's very pretty," Jessica told her trying to sound enthusiastic. It was all ribbons and lace and, she couldn't help thinking, a bit out of character for little tomboy Becky. But Cassandra's taking the time to buy it was a refreshing change. The situation brought to mind the dilemma of Rachael's graduation dress. Perhaps Cassandra had decided to become more attentive to the children.

"Mommy let me try it on to show Agatha before she leaves, and I can keep it on until Daddy gets home. His plane landed already."

Jessica processed the information in Becky's statement. So David had been out of town again. He apparently was traveling more than usual these days. "Where is Agatha going?" She felt a little guilty gleaning information from the child. But she hadn't seen Becky or any of the family in over a week, and she had the strange sensation that she was on the outside looking in at their lives these days.

"She's going to be a grandma. Her daughter's at the hospital now having the baby."

"Oh! How wonderful!" Jessica knew that Agatha's daughter had been expecting Agatha's first grandchild.

Jessica offered Becky cookies and milk, hoping to prolong her stay, but Becky was afraid of soiling her dress. Then her eyes were drawn to the screen door by the sound of a vehicle passing the house.

"Daddy's home! I have to go show him my dress. Bye!" She flew out the door and scurried towards home. Watching her go, Jessie felt a sense of loss and isolation.

Another full week went by, and Jessica saw neither David nor the children. Perhaps, practically speaking, it was for the best, but she missed them terribly.

In a department store that day, waiting to pay for a purchase, she had stood beside an infant and its mother. The infant reached towards Jessica, and without thinking, she had taken his little hand in hers as she spoke to him. The empty ache that she used to feel so often had returned. She realized with a jolt that she hadn't felt that particular ache in a long time, since soon after she'd met Becky. Had Becky been filling that void within her? She wondered now why Becky's visits had grown so infrequent. She hadn't seen her since the day she'd come to show her the new dress.

And David. She hadn't caught as much as a glimpse of him since the night of the party. She had expected to feel lonely once they'd decided not to see each other, but this emptiness was almost more than she could bear. She hadn't seen Rachael, Tad, or Agatha either. She felt cut off totally from most of the friends and companions she'd come to know here.

The only positive aspect in all of this was that, to combat the loneliness, she had submerged herself in her studies. Not only had she caught up, but she'd completed some of the reading assignments for next week. Strangely, she didn't feel the satisfaction she would have expected.

Sitting in her living room as she pondered these happenings, Jessica suddenly realized that someone was knocking at her door. When she opened it, she found a troubled-looking Agatha.

"Jessica, dear, I'm so sorry, but I have to ask a favor of you. I don't know where else to turn."

"What is it, Agatha?" Jessica had never seen the older woman look so troubled.

"It's my daughter. As you probably know, she had a baby girl last week . . ."

"I didn't know it was a girl. Congratulations, Agatha!" She hugged the dear woman and was surprised to receive only a weak hug in return. She held her out at arm's length. "What is it, Agatha? What's wrong?"

Agatha gave her something between a grimace and a smile. "Probably nothing serious, but the baby cried all last night. They assumed it was only a touch of colic, but this morning both my daughter and the baby began running fevers. The doctor said it's just a bacterial infection, but my daughter is exhausted and needs help. I'd like to go over and stay the night so that she can get some sleep."

She looked at Jessica with an apologetic expression. "I hate to ask. I know how busy you are, but David is out of town. Could you possibly stay with the children for one night? I'd come home as early as possible tomorrow."

"Of course. I'll pack a bag and come right over." She could afford one evening, and how fortunate that she just happened to be caught up in both her classes. In truth, she had to admit that spending an evening with the children sounded like fun. "I'll be there in half an hour." Her voice reflected her enthusiasm.

Thirty minutes later, with a small overnight bag, Jessica walked up the Bennington driveway. Agatha stood at the open door of her car, inserting her own small overnight case, and looked up to give Jessica a smile of gratitude. "I think I'm just about ready. I'll call you this evening to see how things are going."

"No need for that," Jessica told her. "If you'll just leave your daughter's telephone number in case we have any questions, that will be fine."

Agatha gave Jessica an enthusiastic hug. "Thank you so much, dear. I've already left the phone number on the counter in the kitchen." She glanced into the car as if checking to see if she had everything. "Well, I'll just run along then. If I don't talk to you tonight, I'll see you in the morning."

Jessica patted her shoulder. "I hope both your daughter and the baby feel better soon.

Later that evening, Jessica, with Rachael's help, fixed hamburgers for dinner. Afterwards they watched a movie and then worked on a puzzle. Jessica enjoyed being with the children again, and found an evening away from study a welcome relief.

When the time came to get ready for bed, Rachael helped Jessica put sheets on the bed in the guest room.

After the older children had gone to bed, and Jessica had tucked Becky in, she walked to the guest room. Before entering, she stopped to look into the bedroom across the hall.

This must be David's room. She took a step inside. The room smelled of his scent. One of his ties lay across the back of a chair, and a shirt hung on a hanger on the doorknob of the closet. His presence seemed to linger in the room, even in his absence.

She looked at his bed, the one in which he slept almost every night, and fought a desire to lie upon it too. Just once, she thought, to feel that closeness to him.

But she turned away and went into the guest room, shutting the door firmly behind her. After putting on her nightgown, she got into bed and decided to read for a while. When reading didn't seem to make her sleepy, she put the book aside and turned off the light.

After a long while, she dozed, but only fitfully.

She awoke with a start to the sound of water running. At first she couldn't remember where she was, then memory flooded back. One of the children must have gotten up, perhaps for a drink of water. After several moments, the sound ceased.

Jessica propped herself up on an elbow, listening intently. After another moment, something bumped and then a shower door slid.

What in the world was going on? Surely one of the children wouldn't get up in the middle of the night and decide to take a shower.

She climbed out of bed and groped for her robe in the darkness. In the process she knocked over a large vase in a nearby corner. It hit the wall with a thud.

Jessica felt for the bedside lamp and turned it on. As she stooped to set the vase upright, she noted that all sound in the house had ceased. Pulling on her robe, her heart beating rapidly, she rushed out into the hallway. Then skidded to a stop.

A light burned in David's bedroom. And the door stood open.

Then suddenly he was walking towards her, tying the cord of navy sweat pants. As he gave it a last tug, he looked up and saw her and stopped dead in his tracks.

"Jessica!" His eyes widened. "I heard a noise. I was going to check on the kids." He shook his head as if to clear it. "What are you doing here?"

He wore only the sweat pants and a T-shirt, which he had apparently pulled on in order to make his check. His hair was damp from the shower. Involuntarily, Jessica took in his well-developed chest and arms, which strained at the seams of his shirt.

Then she looked into his dark eyes and her knees grew weak. She reached for the door jamb to steady herself and struggled to collect her thoughts.

"Uh, Agatha had to leave. Her . . . her daughter is

having problems with the baby," she explained in an unsteady voice.

"I'm sorry to hear that."

"She'll be back tomorrow. We didn't know you'd be home tonight."

"I finished up my business early."

David's gaze slid down over her night clothes, and Jessica pulled her robe more tightly around herself, suddenly self-conscious. "I . . . I can just collect my things and go home."

He smiled. "Don't be silly. It's late."

He couldn't send her packing this time of night. Nor did he want to. Her appraising look and the way it seemed to fluster her thoughts made his own heart race. He looked into her eyes and took a step towards her.

She stepped backward. "Are you hungry? We just had hamburgers for dinner, but I could fix you one."

He shook his head. "I had a meal on the plane."

"Oh. Yes. Of course."

Her wide, brown eyes looked up at him. Her warm full lips parted slightly. Their gazes locked and some force in the atmosphere seemed to contract and pull them together. He reached for her.

Somewhere in the back of his mind, a stubborn voice nagged that he should resist this. But the pull towards her was too strong. The ache to hold her in his arms was irresistible.

When his hand touched her arm, she seemed to

tremble in response, then stepped forward into his embrace. The last remnants of his control crumbled as he pulled her close, and her welcoming arms wound around his neck.

David had lived this scenario so many times in his dreams that he half expected to wake up. But she melted against him, real and warm, and when his mouth descended to hers, her lips moved softly under his own. He kissed her once more and then pulled back to look into her eyes. "I'm so glad you're here," he whispered. "I've missed you so much."

She smiled gently up at him. "I've missed you too, David."

He held her gaze. "Have you?"

She nodded, and David returned her smile. "Maybe we should rethink this business about avoiding each other. Two intelligent people should be able to solve our problems."

Happiness brightened her eyes. "I think so too."

He couldn't pull his gaze from her lips and lowered his mouth to hers again. She responded and clung to him as he deepened their kiss.

Then, through a fog of desire, he heard the click of a nearby door. David groaned and went still. His hands moved to Jessica's shoulders, and he straightened.

"Daddy?" Becky stood in the hallway, rubbing her eyes. "I had a bad dream." The pout on her face turned to a quizzical frown as she looked up at them. "Were you hugging Jessica?"

David gave Jessica the barest hint of a smile as he released her, but not before moving his hands over her shoulders possessively.

He stooped to Becky and smoothed her hair from her face. "Yes, I was hugging Jessica. I haven't seen her in a long time, and I've missed her."

"When did you get home?"

"Just a little while ago. Now, come on, let's get you back in bed."

She took a step away from her own bedroom doorway and eyed it with trepidation. "I had a bad dream. There was a monster in my closet." Her lower lip trembled. "Can I sleep with you?"

David let out a long breath. "Yeah, sure. Go jump in bed, and I'll be right in."

She took a few steps into his room and then looked back at Jessica with an impish grin.

"Can I sleep with Jessica?"

David looked at Jessica, and she laughed. "Sure." She held her hand out to the child. "Come on." Then she looked back at David, still smiling. "Good night."

He winked at them both. "Good night," he mumbled, watching as Jessica led Becky into the bedroom. He saw her tenderness with the child.

How could she be anything but good for all of them? Sure her schooling and potential career were important to her. But she was here—in the middle of the night, taking care of his children. That said something about her priorities, didn't it? Besides, they all needed her. And he couldn't stay away from her any longer.

Jessica awoke the next morning as Becky wiggled out of bed. She struggled to pull herself from sleep and heard movement in other parts of the house.

Memories of the night before flooded back, and Jessica sighed with a happy contentment. Something had happened when she and David embraced last night. They had both silently acknowledged that they needed to be together. She had lain awake for hours after he'd left them, reveling in the memory of his touch and his kiss.

She had waited so long for this, dreamed of it. Both of them together in this house. With the children.

For just a moment, she let herself pretend they were her children. That this was her family.

From the kitchen the sound of clinking glasses interrupted her thoughts. Was everyone else up? Then with a surge of blissful anticipation, she wondered if she could catch David before he left for the office.

Jumping out of bed and pulling on her jeans and shirt, she ran a comb through her hair and hurried out to the kitchen.

She entered to find Rachael and Tad finishing up their bowls of cereal. Someone had apparently gotten Becky a bowl too, and she knelt on a chair, pouring flakes both into her bowl and onto the tabletop.

Then Jessica detected a movement from the other

side of the room. She looked up to see David moving towards her with a soft smile on his face. His "good morning, Jessica" was full of sensuous meaning as he lowered his head to brush his lips against hers.

She warmed instantly in response to his touch and returned his soft look. Then muffled exclamations from the children sent a rush of heat to her cheeks, despite David's reassuring smile. He slid his arm around her waist and pulled her to him, but let the children's questioning looks go unanswered.

After draining his coffee cup, he announced in a reluctant voice that he had to leave. He'd have given anything to stay. All of them here together, having breakfast with the sun streaming in the windows seemed so right. He longed to relish the warm feelings that coursed through him. But duty called.

Jessica accompanied him into the living room, where he picked up his briefcase. He called good-bye to the children and reached for her hand. Stopping at the front door, he lowered his head to kiss her again. Then his arms enfolded her as if they were meant to do so, and he whispered into her ear. "I'll miss you."

"I'll miss you too." Her voice sounded choked with feeling.

He kissed her lightly one last time. "We'll talk tonight. We'll solve this whole situation." She nodded, and as he moved away, he held her hand until the increasing distance between them necessitated his letting go.

She watched him get into his car and waved as he drove away, experiencing a pang of pain at their separation.

When his car had disappeared around the bend, she returned to the kitchen. The children's low, excited chatter ceased as she entered the room. They watched her in curious silence as she poured herself coffee. She joined them at the table and asked questions about their planned day's activities, deciding to leave the answers to their obvious questions to David.

The bright sun coming in the window warmed her, and a contented happiness filled her, sitting here with David's children. She only wished he could have remained with them.

An hour later, Agatha arrived, and soon afterwards, Jessica left for her own home.

She studied for the remainder of the morning and most of the afternoon. As evening approached, she waited to hear from David. She expected either the telephone's ring or his knock at her door at any moment as she ate a light dinner and then sat watching the sunset.

When the sun's brightness had faded from the sky, she still sat waiting. She couldn't help remembering the happy contentment she'd felt, bathing in the rays of this same day's sun as it rose this morning.

Darkness fell and the hour grew late, and still she heard nothing from him. The joy of the previous night and the contentment of the morning faded. The warmth of being held in David's arms now seemed like an unreal dream. She thought of calling him, but by the time she did so, the hands of the clock had inched towards midnight, and she decided it was too late.

She had a study date the next morning, a Saturday, with two of her classmates at the school library. They had decided that preparing for finals together might prove helpful to all of them. And under the circumstances, it was probably for the best, Jessica concluded: She could keep her mind on her studies more effectively there. The study session went about as successfully as she could have hoped, under the circumstances.

She waited all that evening but heard nothing from David. As midnight drew near once again, she couldn't contain her resentment. How could he be this unfeeling? Had he decided their behavior had been too impulsive? If so, he at least owed her an explanation.

She thought of the erratic nature of his behavior towards her from the very beginning. She'd allowed herself to be pulled first one way and then another at his every whim, she told herself. She had, in fact, found it emotionally impossible to do anything else. How weak and foolish she'd acted!

Well, no more. She could never respect herself if she allowed this to continue.

Sunday came and went, and still she heard nothing

from David. All her denunciations of his character and her chastisement of her own hardened into a formidable resolve. Now that she could see the situation clearly, she couldn't believe that she had allowed herself to be manipulated so. She blamed herself more than David: Had she no self-respect at all?

Chapter Eight

Finally, the following evening around sunset, a knock sounded at her front door. She opened it, and found herself facing David. She had stopped expecting him, so his sudden appearance came as a shock.

He looked tired and dark circles ringed his eyes. He wore a sport jacket, but his tie hung loose around an open collar, and his shirt looked as though he'd slept in it. He stood slumped against the doorjamb, and when she opened the door, he moved as if to come in. But she flung an arm across the doorway to block his way.

He gave her a confused, quizzical look. "Aren't you going to let me in?"

"No, David. I don't want to see you."

He looked at her dumbly as though having difficulty

comprehending what she said. Then some realization seemed to dawn on him. "Look, Jessie, I know I haven't been in touch with you, but there's a reason. Let me come in and explain."

"No. I'm through listening to your explanations. Whatever it is this time, I don't want to hear it." She tried to close the door, but his hand moved to stop it.

"Jessica, please. Listen to me."

"No!" She threw her weight against the door, evidently surprising him, because it slammed shut. She quickly threw the dead-bolt into place.

"Jessica! You don't know what you're doing! I've got to talk to you."

"Go home, David."

"Jessica!" He pounded on the door.

She ran down the hall to her bedroom and closed that door too, falling against it. She put her hands over her ears and slumped to the floor. She wasn't sure how long she sat there, but it seemed a very long time. When she let her hands fall to her sides, only the sounds of crickets outside greeted her ears. She remained on the floor for some time, breathing hard, satisfied with herself. She'd done it. And she would continue to refuse to listen to his excuses.

The shrill ring of the telephone startled her. Pulling herself to her feet, she walked to the living room to listen to the answering machine and heard David's voice. "Jessica, I know you're there. Please pick up the phone. You've got to let me explain."

"No, I don't." And she walked back to the bedroom where she couldn't hear anymore. The telephone rang twice more that night, but she stayed in her room and tried to study. She had her last exam in two days, and she resolved to concentrate and do well.

She left for school early the next morning, determined to avoid any chance of David's catching her. And she stayed late, arriving home close to dark.

She had been home only a short time when she heard a knock at her door. Looking covertly through the kitchen window curtain, she saw that it was David again. He knocked a second time, but she walked back to the living room, wringing her hands.

"I know you're in there, Jessica," he called to her. "I'm not leaving until you come out or let me in." After a moment, he knocked again, calling out her name. Then silence fell.

After a while, she stole to the window. He was still out there, pacing back and forth. Returning to the living room, she closed the drapes, in case he should decide to come around to the back. A few moments later, he knocked again. "I'm not leaving, Jessica."

Her sense of indignation flared. She was acting like a trapped animal. She marched to the window, parted the curtain, and looked out at him. "David, if you don't leave, I'll call the police. I mean it."

"All right, Jessie. Just talk to me through the window then."

"No! Go away! Or so help me, David, I will call

them. I'm sick to death of your explanations. I have a legal right to privacy, and I intend to make sure that I get it." She let the curtain fall back into place and stepped back from the window.

David, too, took several steps backward. He had never seen her so angry or so adamant. And he couldn't afford a run-in with the police, especially not now. After a few more moments of pacing in front of her door, he walked back towards his own home.

When she saw him leave, Jessica sighed in bitter satisfaction. Her successful self-assertion added strength to her resolve. Never again would she allow herself to be emotionally manipulated. By David or anyone else.

She had arrived here in Woodsborough with the intention of concentrating on her education and a career, and on avoiding romantic entanglements. She had allowed that resolve to falter. But never again.

Too often during her lifetime, she had allowed her emotions to rule in her response to people, had allowed herself to become involved in their problems. She remembered Jim's words of caution to her on one of these occasions: "Jessie, it's fine to be concerned about other people, but you have to take care of yourself first because no one else is going to do it for you." Well, that was especially true now that Jim was gone: She had to take care of herself. And she would do so.

Her newfound determination and the ease with which she put the distracting influences of the past days out of her mind surprised her. That evening, she had several productive hours of study. Except for one call from a classmate, the telephone remained silent. Perhaps David had given up. Maybe he would leave her alone now.

The following morning, she rose early again. She had just one more study session today and tomorrow her last final. She didn't want to take a chance of a distracting encounter with David. As she headed out the door at seven o'clock, the birds sang in the trees and the air smelled fresh. She really should get out in the early mornings more often, she told herself, turning to lock her door. The dead-bolt had just dropped into place when she heard his voice.

"Jessica."

She tried to push the key back into the lock, but her hand shook. Then his hand covered hers, and he pulled the key away. She turned to him, a ferocity flaring deep inside, but his words, coming quickly to the point, silenced her.

"Cassandra is trying to take Becky away from me, Jessica. Please, I've got to talk to you."

His words stunned her, but she fought to keep her anger from draining away. "That's not my problem, David."

Alarm flickered in his eyes but determination quickly replaced it. "You don't mean that."

"Yes, I do. I have my own problems, and I have to get to school now." She started to turn towards her car, but he put his hand on her arm to stop her. Indignation flared, and she looked first at his hand and then up into his face, eyes blazing.

He snatched his hand away as though the contact had seared him, holding it up as if to imply that he wouldn't touch her again, but the determination in his eyes never faltered. "Jessica, please. We're talking about my life here. We've been friends. You've got to at least listen to me."

"Friends? Is that what we've been?" She shook her head. "I don't think you know the meaning of the word." She started to turn from him again, but thoughts of Becky stopped her. If this was about Becky, perhaps she should listen. But she wouldn't allow him to look into her eyes. And she would keep a cautious wall around her emotions.

"All right," she forced a cooler-than-ever edge into her voice, "tell me what you're so determined to say. But make it brief. I don't have much time." Her study session didn't start until ten o'clock, but he didn't need to know that.

David looked around uncertainly. "Could we at least go into the backyard . . . so that we can sit down."

Wariness pricked at her. "No. I told you that I'm in a hurry. Tell me here and now, or I'm leaving."

"Please, Jessica." She allowed herself a brief glance into his eyes and saw both pain and pleading there. Compassion threatened to cloud her new clarity of judgment, and she pushed it firmly away. She'd listen only so long as this concerned Becky. Holding her head high and her back ramrod straight, she walked silently towards the backyard.

Placing her books on the patio table, she sat in one of the chairs and looked up at David in a business-like manner. He sat down opposite her, visibly tense and apprehensive. He looked tired and his bloodshot eyes still had dark semicircles beneath them. He seemed to study her expression briefly and then began.

"I intended to call you Friday night, Jessica. I looked forward to it all day, but Cassandra called me first." He seemed to shudder at the recollection. "Derek has asked her to marry him. She's been in Boston with him, but told me that she was coming back to California the following day—Saturday—to discuss an important matter with me. I didn't like her tone of voice and thought I'd better be prepared for whatever she had to say. I called my attorney and spent the rest of the evening on the phone and in conference with him."

David paused and seemed to study Jessica's reaction. She gazed back at him with a carefully impassive expression. "When I was finished with all of that," he continued, "it was past midnight and too late to call you.

"I tried once the following morning, but you were gone. I probably should have left a message, but I wasn't thinking clearly." He shifted and, leaning his elbows on his knees, clenched white-knuckled hands together.

"When Cassandra got here late Saturday afternoon, she told me that a prestigious university in Boston had offered Derek an endowed chair. They plan to marry and live on the East Coast. Cassandra will practice law, but she also has an urge to play mother again." David paused and took a fortifying breath. "She's suing me for custody of Becky."

Despite the fact that she'd known what was coming, Jessica couldn't suppress a small gasp.

"Cassandra and Derek both think they have a good chance of gaining custody," David continued. "Becky's very young and without a mother now. They feel that the two-parent home they could offer her would work heavily in their favor."

David stared down at his clenched fists. "Cassandra has first-hand knowledge of how many hours I work and how much I travel." His gaze rose to meet Jessica's. "And she also found out about the day Becky disappeared. That I was taking care of her but working in my office." He paused and drew a deep breath. "So that's where things stand now.

"I've been beside myself, Jessie. I've been talking to lawyers and everyone else I could think of who could give me advice on the subject. That's why I didn't get over here until Monday. I'm sorry. I should have contacted you sooner."

Jessica saw the deep lines of worry in his face and

fought to keep a wall around her own emotions, telling herself that whatever the facts, this man's foremost intention today was to explain away his ill-treatment of her once again. She refused to consider the possibility that she was being unreasonable. Besides, she thought with an iota of relief, wasn't he making the situation sound more serious than it was?

"I can't believe that any judge would give Cassandra custody of Becky," she told him in a crisp tone. "She deserted the family years ago. And Becky and Cassandra have never been close. Cassandra has taken very little interest in the children for years."

"But she has taken an interest in Becky lately. Cassandra's been playing up to her: buying her things, taking her places." Jessica remembered the frilly dress Becky had come over to show her.

"Becky was never as traumatized by the separation as the older two," David continued. "She was so young when Cassandra left, she's hardly known anything else."

"But surely if a judge asked her whom she'd rather live with, she'd choose you."

"Maybe. But she'd also probably tell him that she was fond of her mother."

Jessica had to admit that might be true, but she also told herself it wasn't her problem. Now that the protective wall surrounded her emotions, she refused to let it fall. She was safer this way. Her feelings for David had been so strong that they had obscured her objectivity. Had made her ignore all of the cautions and resolves she'd set up for herself after Jim's death. She squared her shoulders and met David's gaze with as cool a demeanor as she could muster.

"So now I understand why you haven't contacted me, and I forgive you. Can I go to class now?"

"There's more, Jessie."

She had begun to rise but sank back into her chair with an air of irritability. "What is it?"

David got up and began to pace, looking both desperate and frustrated. "God, Jessica, you're not in the right frame of mind for this." Then he turned to look at her. "But I don't have any choice. I don't have much time." He walked back to his chair and pulled it close to hers. He sat down facing her and took her hands in his. She tried to pull away, but he held fast. "Please, Jessica. Just for a moment. Just listen."

Her heart thudded in her chest, and she ceased the useless struggle to free her hands. "Then hurry and get it over with," she ordered in a flat, emotionless voice.

A worried look crossed David's features before the pleading returned to his eyes. He swallowed hard.

"Will you marry me, Jessica?"

Her mouth dropped open in surprise. Her thoughts raced wildly, analyzing everything he'd told her. *He was asking her to help him provide a two-parent home for Becky. In order to neutralize Cassandra's advantage.*

Jessica pulled her hands from his. She stood and

moved away. After several moments, she turned to him, indignant and hurt. "You would really use me this way?"

His gaze flickered away from hers and then came back. "That's not the way it is, Jessica."

She continued as if he hadn't spoken. "But, of course, you would. For Becky. I don't know why that should surprise me."

David stood and moved as if to approach her, but she stepped back, giving him a warning look, and he stopped. "You must know that I'm in love with you."

"Love?" She laughed in utter disillusionment. "No, David. That's the first time you've used the word. You've said that you needed me or that you wanted me, but never that you loved me. Only now when the word suits your purpose. Is this what your attorneys advised you to do? To get married right away? To just anyone if necessary? And have you been carrying on consultations all weekend trying to find another way out?"

"Jessica, you've got to believe me. I do love you. It's true that I've been trying to find other grounds to keep Becky, but only because I didn't want to ask you to marry me under these circumstances." His eyes softened. "After Friday night, I knew I couldn't live without you anymore. I decided then to ask you to marry me. You can't deny the strong feelings that exist between us."

She squared her shoulders and held her head high.

"They don't exist anymore, David. Not for me. You see, I've come over to your way of thinking. Too many differences in needs and lifestyle exist between us. You view with suspicion any woman who wants a career and see her as a threat to the stability of your family.

"But I need to establish a career for myself. Need to know that if I'm ever left alone again, I can take care of myself.

"And I'm still afraid of abandoning myself to love again. I don't think I'll ever lose the fear that it could all be taken away from me again in one horrible catastrophe. Your not calling me for several days brought that fear alive again."

"Listen to me, sweetheart, I was wrong about our differences. I've watched you keep up with your class work and make time for the children too. I've watched you put them ahead of your work when necessary, even though it means hectic weeks of catching up." He paused and his voice dropped an octave. "I trust you, Jessica. With my own life and the lives of my children. We want you. We love you."

"Because I'm your only option right now."

"That not true! And it's not fair!"

She shook her head. "You're wasting your time, David. I won't marry you. But you'll do fine without me. And in the end, you'll be glad that you did. Someday you'll find someone with whom you're more compatible.

"Now if you'll excuse me, I can't afford any more distractions. I have to get to school." She picked up her books and walked rapidly towards the front of the house and her car.

He let her go. Trying to talk to her when she was in this frame of mind wouldn't do any good.

If only Cassandra had waited a few more weeks before she dropped this bombshell. By then, he'd have asked Jessica to marry him, and she'd have no reason to be suspicious of his motives.

Because he did love her. God, how he loved her. The thought of going through life without her now seemed unbearable.

Without either Jessica or Becky.

The thought left him feeling bereft. He sat down heavily in a chair and covered his eyes with his hands. Oh, please, no.

Jessica sifted through the contents of the mailbox and her eager hands snatched up the postcards. Both of her grade results had arrived. Her gaze flew over them, and she breathed a sigh of relief. She had done better than she dared hope.

Exams had been over for more than a week. Since finishing her last one, Jessica had kept busy around her house. She had shopped for new shades for the room she intended making into her office. Once she had her degree and had begun making money, she hoped to get a new, more up-to-date computer. Then that would be the room in which she hoped to do some freelance writing and possibly even start her novel— in her spare time and on weekends, of course. She found herself thinking more and more about career plans and the future. Perhaps because she was trying to keep her mind off present circumstances.

She hadn't seen David and the children in weeks. The last time she'd seen David was the morning he had proposed marriage to her, over two weeks ago. Becky had stopped in to see her once, but Jessica had been on her way out and didn't have time to visit.

She'd learned from Pat that David had taken the children on a short vacation this past week. A friend who had a house at the beach had loaned it to them, and they'd gone, planning to do some swimming and boating.

At first Jessica enjoyed the total quiet, but in the last day or two, she had begun to feel lonely. She'd played tennis with Pat once and had plans to play with her again tomorrow, but that and shopping was not enough to fill her days. She had considered going to Colesville again, but her mother's college roommate had been visiting from the East Coast. Perhaps she'd go in a few days.

She wasn't sure what to expect once David returned. He hadn't attempted to contact her at all during her exams or before he left on vacation.

Pat had told her that Cassandra was still intent on taking Becky to Massachusetts to live with her and

that David was equally determined that she would not.
Their attorneys were battling it out. Pat had eyed Jessica almost accusingly when she'd said that, but Jessie
had changed the subject. Her mind was made up, and
she didn't want anyone trying to convince her to
change it. She was sure that David would succeed in
keeping Becky with himself without her help. After
all, she reminded herself again, Cassandra had left all
of them several years ago.

The next morning, Pat picked Jessica up for tennis.
The morning was cool and pleasant, and Jessica
looked forward to the game. As the car exited her
driveway and headed towards the club, she noticed the
Bennington wagon in the driveway. They were home
again. The rush of excitement she experienced surprised and dismayed her.

Later at the tennis club, as they were beginning their
second set, Jessica noticed four men enter a court
nearby. Brad and David were among them. Pat waved,
and when the men did likewise, Jessica also waved
weakly.

Her own reaction to the sight of David distressed
her. Her pulse began to race, and between each of the
next several points, her eyes kept going back to him.
Her stomach did a little flip each time she caught sight
of him.

As a result, she and Pat lost the next several games.
Angry, Jessica reprimanded herself. She had made her

decision, and she had to stick to it. She wouldn't settle for a marriage of convenience. Such a tenuous relationship would almost certainly fail, and once they had become a family, she knew she couldn't take losing them all again. And it would be disastrous for the children. She had made the only wise decision and would stick to it.

She began to succeed in erecting the wall around her emotions once again. She even played better. She and Pat lost but only by a couple of games. They played one more set and lost again but this time in a tie break.

When they had finished, Jessica wanted to leave. The more distance she put between herself and David the better. But the other women seemed inclined to talk, and since Pat had driven, Jessica had no choice but to stay until they had run out of conversation. She did keep her eyes, if not her mind, off the men's court, however.

When finally they walked through the parking lot towards Pat's car, they heard someone call Pat's name and turned to see David approach. Jessica unconsciously straightened as he drew closer and watched him anxiously. The nearer he came, the more she felt her protective reserve slipping.

He looked wonderful. He sported a deep tan, the result of his week at the beach, she supposed. His hazel eyes looked dark with intensity as his gaze darted between Pat and herself. When he stopped a few feet from them, Jessica caught the scent of his after-shave, and it aroused the familiar primitive instinct, which she struggled to subdue. Her response to him alarmed her, and she frantically reminded herself not to let him manipulate her again.

David spoke to Pat. "Would you mind if I took Jessica home. I'd like to talk to her."

"No!" Jessica heard the note of panic in her own voice. "We don't have anything to talk about."

His eyes fixed on her intently. "I think we do, Jessica."

"I'm sorry, but I'm going with Pat." But when she turned, she saw that Pat was already several feet away and getting into her car. She moved quickly to follow, but David's hand gripped her arm.

"Please, Jessica."

She wrenched her arm from his grasp just as she heard Pat's car start. She watched it move off helplessly, then turned to David in a fit of pique. "All right then, I'll walk home."

"Jessica, be reasonable."

"I thought I'd been reasonable in the past, and only succeeded in making a fool of myself."

He watched her for a moment as her breathing heaved deeply. "All right, we won't talk. But it's my fault you're stranded here, so at least let me take you home." When she started to protest, he reiterated soberly, "I promise I won't say a word."

Drawing a deep breath to calm her emotions, Jessica

proceeded in the direction he indicated, towards his car. He unlocked and opened the door for her, stowing her tennis bag in the back seat. He got in and started the car, all in silence.

Jessica stared straight ahead. She felt him pause to look at her before he put the car in gear and maneuvered it slowly out of the parking lot.

As they turned out onto the road and the car picked up speed, she felt him look at her again. She turned her head away to look out the side window. As promised, they continued on in silence.

Jessica jumped from the car the moment they stopped in front of her house. She wasn't angry anymore so much as worried about succumbing to him should he try another overture.

David got out of the car too, apparently to help her extract her tennis bag from the back seat, but she'd yanked it out before he got around to her side of the car. She glanced at him only for a second. "Good-bye, David."

He didn't answer, but she could feel him watching her until she had unlocked her door. She stepped inside, but before she could close the door, he spoke.

"I love you, Jessica."

She shut the door quietly behind herself, slumping against it. She didn't turn around to look out the window, but in a moment, she heard his car start. As the sound of the engine died away, she felt hot tears slip down her cheeks. A moment later, she sunk into a nearby chair, sobbing uncontrollably. All the pent-up emotion of the past weeks came flooding out with her tears. She cried until she felt exhausted and drained. Then she went to the stove to make herself some tea. Tea always made her feel better.

As the heating water rumbled in the teapot, a feeble knock sounded at her door. Wiping away the remnants of tears, she peered out the window. Her gaze started high and then dropped until she encountered the vision of Becky, gripping something tightly in her fists. Wiping her cheeks once more and taking a deep breath, Jessica strode to the door and opened it.

Becky smiled up at her. "I brought you something from the beach." She proudly handed Jessica a plastic bag full of shells. Jessica's voice broke as she invited Becky in, and the little girl studied her with a frown. "Are you crying?"

Ignoring the question, Jessica lifted the bag of shells to eye level. "Did you gather these yourself?"

Becky nodded. "Spill them out on the table and look at them. They're pretty."

Jessica walked on shaky legs to the table and poured the contents of the bag onto a place mat. As she listened to a litany of the sites the child had found each shell, tears slid down Jessica's cheeks once again.

Chapter Nine

"Jessica's crying." David looked up from the paper he had been trying unsuccessfully to read as Becky came into the room.

"She's crying now?"

Becky nodded. "She said she liked my shells and that they didn't make her cry. Then she hugged me."

A cautious, questioning hope rose slowly in David's breast. Had her crying anything to do with him? Or was she anticipating Becky's possible departure from them all? He knew Jessica loved Becky and the other children as well. Maybe someday she would allow herself to love him again. But she was holding back now, denying any feelings she'd had for him. He prayed that time and consideration would someday prompt her to allow herself to come to him.

Because he did love her. Undeniably. Even during all the legal conferences, the worry over the possible loss of Becky, the arguments with Cassandra, he couldn't rid himself of the emotional emptiness her absence left within him.

And at the beach, he had tried to join enthusiastically in the children's fun. But even among the four of them, things weren't quite right without her. Her presence supplied a warmth and cohesion they all needed now.

That one short experience with holding her at night and having her with them at breakfast in the morning had confirmed his conviction of how beautiful life could be with her. He vowed to fight with all the intellectual and emotional resources he possessed and with all the legal help that money could buy to make the five of them a family.

Once Becky had left, Jessica's tears flowed freely again. She knew they were tears of farewell—to both David and Becky. This was the way things had to be, and she must learn to accept them. She worked in her garden for the next hour to calm her nerves.

Late in the afternoon, the telephone rang.

"Jessica? It's me." Jessica recognized her mother's voice, but it sounded thin and strained, not at all her usual cheerful self. Jessica's stomach tightened into a knot.

"What's wrong, Mom?"

"It's your father, dear. He's in the hospital."

Jessica lowered herself unsteadily into a chair. "What happened?" Even as she asked the question, she feared the answer. Her mother wouldn't sound this way unless it were serious.

Her mother's voice wavered with emotion, and Jessica could tell that she was on the verge of tears. "He's had a heart attack, honey."

Jessica gripped the edge of the table and beads of perspiration formed on her forehead. She felt almost as though she might faint.

"How serious is it?"

"The doctor's aren't sure yet. They're doing some tests now. I just brought him in a short while ago."

"I'll get there as fast as I can, Mom."

"Be careful driving, honey." And then after a worried pause. "Isn't there someone who could bring you? Maybe you shouldn't drive when you're upset."

"I'm okay, Mom. Don't worry. I'll be careful." She willed herself to calm down. She had to be strong for her mother's sake and in order to do what was necessary. "I'll be there soon."

She hastened to her bedroom and packed a bag. Then she telephoned Pat with trembling fingers.

"Pat, my father's had a heart attack." She heard her voice quaver and clamped her mouth shut.

"Oh, Jess. What can I do?"

"I'm leaving for Colesville now. Will you keep an

eye on things here for me . . . mail, paper, water my plants?"

"Of course, Jessie. Are you all right though? Would you like me to drive you?"

Jessica breathed deeply, steadying both her voice and her emotions. "No, thanks, Pat. I'm all right. I'll leave a key for you under the door mat." She also left Pat her parents' telephone number in case she needed to reach her.

Jessica drove right at the speed limit the entire way. She knew she shouldn't drive any faster because of the precarious state of her nerves, and she couldn't make herself drive slower. She drove on past Colesville to the hospital in the nearby larger town.

Upon entering the hospital, she was directed to the Cardiac Care Unit. She identified herself to the attending nurse, who indicated a room immediately off the nurses' station. Jessica stepped to the doorway.

Her father lay in a bed just a few feet inside the door. His upper body was propped up on pillows, his skin almost as white as the sheets upon which he rested. Tubes connected him to a heart monitor and an intravenous solution ran into his left arm. He appeared to be sleeping.

Her mother sat in a chair at his bedside and looked up as Jessica entered. She came to meet her and stepped out into the hall with her.

Jessica watched her mother wordlessly, afraid to ask the questions uppermost in her mind.

"The doctor just left, honey. He said the next twenty-four hours are the most critical, but that it was a fairly mild attack. They've given him a sedative and want him to rest now, and they'll keep him here for the night. If everything goes well, they may move him to a semi-private room in a day or so."

Jessica allowed a cautious relief to lessen her worry. "Can I see him?"

Her mother gave her a weakly reassuring smile. She reached for Jessica's hand and squeezed it, and then led her back into the room.

Jessica's anxious eyes took in her father's form. He looked so small and vulnerable. And when had his hair gotten so gray? She saw lines in his face that she had never noticed before. But he wasn't old; he wasn't even sixty yet. How could this have happened? He had always seemed so healthy. As these thoughts raced through her mind, his eyes fluttered open and rested on her in recognition.

He struggled to speak. "Hi, honey." His voice sounded hoarse and weak. He tried to smile. "Sorry to bring you all this way. . . ."

She stepped to his side quickly and grasped his hand to silence him. "Shh . . . don't talk, Dad. The doctor wants you to rest. We can talk in the morning."

His eyes fluttered and then closed again. His grasp on her hand loosened. Fear shot through her. She wanted to shake him awake again, make him talk so that she could see that he was all right. But then she saw his chest rise and fall rhythmically in sleep, and her fear lessened, but only a bit. He had seemed so weak, he who had always been the rock of strength in the family. She felt her mother watching her.

"He seems better," the older woman whispered. "He's not having any pain anymore."

Jessica pulled up another chair and they both sank down. They sat watching her father anxiously for what seemed a long time, exchanging whispered conversation from time to time about nothing in particular.

Sometime later, they detected movement in the doorway and looked up to see the doctor. He beckoned to them.

When they stepped out into the hall, he told them that he was pleased with his patient's progress. His vital signs had stabilized, and he seemed to be resting comfortably. He would probably sleep all night. The kindly gray-haired man, probably older than her father, Jessica thought, then suggested that the two women go home and get some sleep too.

They went to a restaurant for a late dinner, although neither felt hungry nor ate very much. Jessica asked to stop at the bookstore before going home. She wasn't sure why; perhaps it was a need to see that some things remained the same.

Back at her parent's home, Jessica watched her mother as she prepared hot milk for both of them. She was still an attractive woman, Jessica thought, slender and vivacious, despite the liberal sprinkling of gray in her dark hair. The observation was comforting and somehow made Jessica feel strong enough to hear the details of her father's heart attack.

"When did it happen, Mom? Where was he?"

"At the store. He called me himself to tell me that he felt strange . . . heaviness in his chest, perspiring, nausea. I called the doctor, and he sent an ambulance to take him to the hospital immediately."

Jessica's parents owned a new and used bookstore in an area of town that had been restored to resemble quaint shops of the past century. Jessica had worked in the store after school during her high-school years, and it was here that she had developed her love for books and her interest in writing.

"The summer is our busiest time, as you know," her mother continued. "One of the new summer people quit a few weeks ago, and Simon hasn't been well and is only working part time." Simon was an old friend of her father's, a teacher who had helped out during the summers for as long as Jessica could remember. "As a result, your dad's been working twelve-hour days, six or seven days a week for most of the summer. Plus he's been having trouble with one of his suppliers. I guess it just got to be too much for him."

Jessica felt a pang of guilt. Perhaps she should have stayed here to help her parents instead of going to school.

Her mother read her thoughts. "Now don't even

think that Jessie, you have to study to do what you love. We'll work things out here."

Jessica nodded, but she wasn't convinced. Maybe this was where she belonged after all.

They drank their milk and talked for another hour. Jessica told her mother that she would stay and help out at the bookstore until they found at least one more full-time person. School didn't start again for over a month, and by that time, the busy summer season would be over. Perhaps she could even come and help out over weekends after that.

When they got to the Cardiac Care Unit at the hospital the next morning, Jessica's father seemed much improved. His color looked better, and he smiled at them as they entered. He was still connected to the heart monitor, but the intravenous tube no longer protruded from his arm. The nurses had told him they would move him to a semi-private room later that day.

They spent the day with him and helped move him to his new room late that afternoon. In the evening, Jessica and her mother accepted an invitation to the home of an old family friend for dinner.

Late on the third afternoon after Jessica's arrival, they all sat talking in her father's room. No one occupied the other bed, so they were alone. Her father continued to improve, and both her parents seemed in good spirits. Jessica, however, couldn't help eyeing her father worriedly from time to time. They'd begun discussing Jessica's decision to stay for several weeks to help out at the bookstore when Jessica saw her mother look towards the doorway and then smile.

Her back to the door, Jessica turned and then sprang to her feet. "David!"

He smiled and nodded at both her parents. Then his eyes came back to Jessica and clouded with concern. "I'm sorry, Jess, but I had to come. We were worried about you." His gaze flickered towards her father and back again to her, and a hint of a smile played on his lips. "But I understand the situation is improving rapidly here."

Jessica was too stunned for a moment to speak. David. Here. She had a strange feeling of the blending of her two different worlds.

Then she realized that everyone was staring at her. Of course, she thought, they don't know each other. Collecting herself, she hurriedly introduced them.

David smiled and nodded to each of them. "Henry. Carolyn."

Jessica explained that David and his family lived next door to her in Woodsborough.

"Oh yes, Jessica has mentioned you and your children many times. It's so nice to finally meet you." Jessica's mother extended her hand to David.

He seemed to take it gratefully and said that he was happy to meet them too. He extended the same hand to Jessica's father.

"Jessica has spoken so well of your children. She's very fond of them as you must know."

David thanked her mother, and said that he was proud of his children. Then his eyes came back to Jessica, and he spoke with a soft intimacy. "Both Pat and I have tried to call you at your parents' home several times. When we couldn't reach you, we became worried."

Jessica felt the self-discipline she'd been exerting over her own feelings the past few days threaten to ebb away. She fought an overwhelming desire to crumple into David's arms. She had to remind herself that this was the man who couldn't decide how he felt about her and then would have used her affection for his own purposes.

She pulled herself upright and explained that she and her mother had been out late both nights since she arrived. But then she gave him a puzzled look. "How did you find us here?"

He explained that Pat remembered the name of the bookstore, and he had gone there. They'd directed him to the hospital.

David addressed his next words to Jessica's father. He commended him on the attractive appearance of the bookstore and on the wide selection of both new and used books. He expressed a desire to spend a little more time there to look around more thoroughly. Soon the two men became engrossed in a discussion about the problems of starting a small business and keeping it going. Each told the other a little about their own experiences.

Jessica looked at her mother in amazement. Her father and David seemed to be hitting it off beautifully. And for some reason that Jessica couldn't fathom, her mother's eyes sparkled with amusement.

Soon afterwards, her father's dinner tray arrived. They had been with him all day, and he had begun to look tired. They would leave him now so that he could rest after dinner, they told him, and would return the next morning. As Jessica kissed her father good-bye, he squeezed her hand and whispered, "I like your young man."

Jessica's eyes widened. "No, Dad . . . he's not . . ." and then she thought better of trying to explain. She returned the squeeze and smiled. "I'll see you in the morning."

As they walked towards the elevator, to Jessica's consternation, she heard her mother invite David to dinner. "We're just having a chicken casserole that I took out of the freezer this morning, but you're welcome to join us."

He accepted the invitation, seemingly with pleasure.

When they arrived at the house, David asked to look around the yard. He admired the big old cherry tree and her mother's carefully cultivated flower beds. Her parent's large, white wood-frame farmhouse was on one acre of what had once been her grandfather's farm. Uninterested in farming, her father had kept the house but sold some of the property. Her Uncle Mel farmed the remaining acres a short distance away.

David listened with interest to her mother's short rendition of this family history. Then going inside, he admired the heavy oak moldings and massive stairway banister in the old house. He looked at Jessica thoughtfully and declared that his visit here explained a lot of her tastes to him—her love of old structures and of books and writing.

She had been watching him intently and felt herself in danger of slipping under his spell once again. But then she reasserted herself. She suddenly resented the way he had injected himself into her life here. This was the place where she had felt safe from his influence, had been able to return from the often painful present to the safe past. She was suddenly angry with her mother too for inviting him here. She felt David watching her. He seemed to sense her abrupt changes in mood.

At dinner, her mother asked a multitude of questions about the children, and David willingly answered them. It was apparent from his remarks that he was very proud of them. Jessica considered their attributes and conceded that he had a right to be proud. He had made it possible for them to become wonderful young people under very difficult circumstances.

Thinking of them, she felt again the pull between her two worlds. She realized again how fond she had become of them. She found herself injecting stories of her own, telling her mother about Becky's precocious paintings and the seashells she'd brought her from the beach.

Her mother looked at her fondly. "This is good for you, isn't it, honey. You've always loved children and wanted your own so badly."

Her mother's words sobered her. No. She wasn't acting as though they were her own. They were merely admirable children.

Her gaze flew to David. Please tell her that's so, she wanted to say.

But he only watched her in silence, furrow lines creasing his forehead. God, why hadn't someone told him this sooner—that her primary desire had always been for a family. Maybe he wouldn't have acted like such a stubborn fool for so long. Their gazes held for several moments until Jessica's mother cleared her throat and offered them dessert. She had taken a cherry pie from the freezer that morning and taken it out of the oven just as they'd started eating. It had cooled enough to eat now.

Jessica felt the irritation flit across her face. She wanted David to leave before her emotions became any more confused. Why was her mother prolonging this? She'd probably ask him to spend the night next.

And to her horror, the next moment, she heard her mother do just that. It was getting dark, and it was such a long drive back to the Bay Area. None of the country roads had lights, she said. When David protested that he had brought no shaver or toothbrush, she insisted they had both with which they could provide him.

David's eyes moved to Jessica's again and held. "I don't think Jessica wants me to stay."

Now it was her mother's turn to show irritation. "Of course, she does. You came here over concern for her. Now it's late, and you're tired. I'm sure she wouldn't want you to take unnecessary risks in driving such a long distance in the dark." She looked at Jessica sternly. "Would you, Jessica?"

Jessica felt her mother's righteous chastisement. These were not the manners she'd been taught as a child in this very hospitable family. Her gaze fell to the table and she spoke quietly. "No. Of course not." She raised her gaze to meet his, "You're welcome to stay, David."

He knew he should leave. She didn't want him here. But now that he had the opportunity, he knew he'd stay. He'd gotten such insight today into how she'd become the Jessica he knew and loved that he couldn't pull himself away yet. Couldn't pull himself away from a chance to spend another night under the same roof with her. He thanked them both and agreed to remain but said he'd have to leave very early the next morning.

They ate their pie and her mother and David talked amicably. He helped them clear the dishes. Then her mother went upstairs to open the windows in the guest room and to get David the articles he needed.

After she'd gone, they moved into the living room. Jessica felt David's gaze upon her, and when she could no longer avoid it, she looked up at him. He smiled wanly. "I promise I'll leave before you get up in the morning."

Again she felt ashamed and, to her chagrin, tears stung her eyes. She turned away, but not before he'd seen them. He moved closely behind her and spoke quietly. "I'm sorry. I didn't mean to upset you more than you already are. I wouldn't have come if I'd known. But we were worried about you, Jessie. We couldn't reach you."

She bit her lower lip and nodded silently.

He willed himself not to reach for her. He wanted to take her in his arms. Hold her. Comfort her. Take care of her. She was so vulnerable right now—and at the same time, so stubbornly strong.

They both heard her mother returning and Jessica hastily wiped away her tears. It had taken all her self-discipline to keep from turning to David and moving into his arms.

Now her mother entered the room and handed David the articles he needed. He thanked her and, declared his intent to retire immediately. He'd have to get up at dawn for his drive back to the Bay Area, he said. He had early meetings. He bade Jessica good night, and then her mother showed him to his room.

Jessica still paced the living room when her mother came back downstairs. The older woman paused and stood watching Jessica thoughtfully. "You're in love with this young man, aren't you, Jessica?"

Jessica's troubled eyes flew to her mother. "No!" But even she wasn't persuaded by the lack of conviction in her response.

Her mother continued to watch her and shook her head. "Jessica, I'm your mother. I know you. The only other man you've looked at in that way was Jim."

Jessica looked away, wringing her hands. "There are extenuating circumstances, Mom. I don't think David feels the same way."

"Then you're a blind young woman. Why, he looks at you almost with . . . reverence." She paused, still watching her daughter intently. "Are you sure you know what you're doing, rebuffing him this way? Judging by everything you've told us about him in the past, he sounds like a very admirable young man." When Jessica didn't answer, because she wasn't sure of the answer herself, her mother questioned her further. "Is it his marriage? What you've told us is true, isn't it? His first marriage is over?"

"Yes, of course. They've been divorced for years."

After a few more moments of silence, her mother spoke again. "I guess you're not going to tell me what the problem is. But may I admonish you to think it through very carefully before you reject this relationship."

Jessica turned to her mother with troubled eyes. "I'll tell you about it, Mom. Just not tonight, okay?"

Her mother nodded and came over to hug her. "Why don't you get some sleep now."

But Jessica didn't sleep much that night, and towards dawn, she heard David moving around in the room next door. She stayed in bed.

Soon he went downstairs. Then for a short while, she heard the hum of voices. Her mother must have gotten up too, probably to see that David didn't leave without breakfast.

Jessica heard the front door close, and she jumped out of bed and moved to the lace-curtained window. She watched as David got into his car and started it, and then as its exhaust dissolved into the cool morning air. As the car moved away, a sense of loss and loneliness seized her, and she wanted to run after him, beg him not to leave her.

Then in the next moment, her sudden mood swings and confused attitude towards him irritated her. She knew what was right and necessary for herself, and she had to stick by it. But now even her mother had begun to undermine her resolve.

Jessica's father continued to improve and in less than a week came home from the hospital. Jessica stayed and helped out at the bookstore for another three weeks.

Through word of mouth, she and her mother found another employee for the bookstore: a middle-aged woman whose children had recently gone out on their own who was looking for a full-time job. She loved books and expressed excitement about working at the bookstore. And as Jessica observed their immediate rapport, she decided that the woman might prove to be a companion for her mother, who also helped out at the store.

On Jessica's last night at home, and after her father had gone to bed, she and her mother sat talking. Jessica finally poured out the story of the relationship between herself and David.

Her mother told her that she understood her fears and that she remembered well Jessie's resolve never to fall in love again and to gain and retain financial and emotional independence. She spoke to her gently now.

"Honey, whenever we allow ourselves to care for someone, we take a chance of being hurt. You love your father and me, but someday we'll be gone. And you'll hurt. And if you have no one else, how much more painful that will be. You have no brothers or sisters.

"Only you can decide if this particular relationship is right for you, but please try and keep your fears under control while you do. You've always been such a warm, caring person. You need people. A young woman these days can enjoy the love of a family and still retain a sense of independence."

Jessica promised to think about her mother's words and left for Woodsborough the next morning, promising to call during the week and come back the following weekend.

They watched in silence as the young waitress placed their luncheon plates and cups of coffee before them. After a few words about the appetizing appearance of the food, they began to eat.

Jessica had been home for three days now, and today, she and Pat had gone out on an old-fashioned shopping excursion. They'd each bought a couple of items of clothing and now had stopped for lunch in one of the department store tea rooms.

Jessica had just begun to lift her second forkful of Chinese chicken salad to her mouth when Pat's words arrested her motion in midair.

"Did you know that the hearing for Becky's custody comes up in just two days?"

Jessica looked at her friend dumbstruck. Until now, the thought that David might lose custody of Becky had seemed an abstract possibility. But somehow, the news of the imminence of the upcoming hearing made the danger seem real and immediate.

Jessica's initial reaction came in the form of panic for both David and Becky. If it came to that, how would David endure having his youngest daughter taken from him after raising her since infancy? His devotion and tender feelings for her were apparent whenever they were together.

And how would Becky endure being taken from her father, brother, and sister to strange surroundings with a mother whose devotion was questionable and a stepfather whom she hardly knew?

Jessica calmed her emotions by assuring herself again that no logical mind would take a child from a secure and loving home and place her in an uncertain situation. Besides, the Bennington family's plight wasn't her problem, she reminded herself. She couldn't and wouldn't assume the responsibility of sacrificing her own well-being to their cause. She wished them well, but she had her own problems.

"No, I didn't know," she told Pat. "I hope all goes well for them." She continued eating in silence, but could have been eating cotton for all she knew.

Pat sighed in loud frustration. "For heaven's sake, Jessica, he's in love with you, and he needs you. You must know that. And you've admitted to me that you care for him too. Why are you doing this? Why won't you at least talk to him?"

Jessica remained staring down at her salad, which she began pushing around the plate with her fork. "Please, Pat, I don't want to talk about it."

Chapter Ten

But at home that evening, Jessica couldn't be quite so calm or philosophical. She paced her living room.

Two days! So little time! And she supposed that once the decision regarding Becky's custody was made, a reversal would prove very difficult.

If she could only believe that David truly loved her, she would happily marry him. She knew that if she let herself, she could very easily fall in love with him.

Jessica groaned. Oh God, she was in love with him now. She had to be honest with herself. But could she trust him? Everyone kept telling her that he loved her. The problem was she couldn't remember David or anyone else ever saying so before this custody issue came up. She had to admit there'd always been an attraction between them, but lust and love were two different things.

Jessica's emotions and her logic tore her first one way and then another until she became almost physically ill. She went to bed but couldn't fall asleep. Towards dawn, she dozed fitfully.

When the sun rose and brightened into daylight, she despaired of sleeping and got up. As she pulled on her robe, she caught a glimpse of her haggard appearance in the mirror, her eyes dark-ringed and bloodshot.

She walked down the hall toward the kitchen and felt a tightening in her chest. *Tomorrow*, she thought. Now the day for the hearing was only one day away.

After a cup of coffee and two tasteless bites of cereal, she decided to clean the house to keep busy. Her frantic concern for David and Becky had her in a state of extreme anxiety, and work might use up some of her nervous energy. She vacuumed the living room, her bedroom, and her future office.

At noon, she sat down to lunch but only stared at her food. Her conversation with David the morning they'd argued in her backyard drifted back. "I was wrong," he'd told her about his distrust of her career aspirations. "I've watched you keep up with your class work and make time for both me and my children too. I trust you . . . want you . . . love you."

Did she also want and need David and his children? Could she trust his explanation of his actions? Trust that he really cared for her? He'd come all the way to Colesville out of concern for her. Had taken a genuine interest in the place and circumstances that had molded her. Didn't that mean something?

And her mother had formed an immediate fondness for him. Jessica had always considered her mother an excellent judge of character. The older woman's words also came back to Jessica: "Whenever we allow ourselves to care for someone, we take a chance of being hurt . . . A young woman these days can enjoy the love of a family and still retain a sense of independence." And her mother claimed to have seen love in both Jessie's and David's eyes.

Jessica fought against letting these memories and opinions sway her. She had to make and live with her own decisions, she told herself.

She tried to consider the situation objectively. She had to admit she'd been in love with David for a long time, but could she really trust him? When she thought back over the months they'd known each other, she couldn't remember one time that he'd lied to her. Why then had she automatically assumed that he'd lied about the reason and timing of his marriage proposal? Had she fought a commitment because of her fear of the risks inherent in giving herself to love?

Closing her eyes, she tried to objectively analyze her feelings. When she thought of what life would be like with David and the children—together every day and every night—an intense joy filled her. Then when she considered the alternative of a life without them, desolation overwhelmed her.

Her eyes flew open. The decision burst upon her and a sense of joy suffused her. She wanted him! Wanted them!

Jessica began to pace. She had to call David. Now! Immediately!

The next moment, fear descended upon her. Would he still want her? Could he forgive her repeated rejection of him?

She had to find out. Her fingers trembled as she reached for the telephone.

But in the next moment, she pulled her hand away. He wouldn't be at home now; he would surely be at the office in the middle of the day. Should she call him there or just leave word at home asking him to call her? She decided to start with his home.

Agatha answered the telephone and told her that David was indeed at work. Jessica left a message asking him to call.

After hanging up, she paced the floor. Would she contact him soon enough this way? Mightn't he have meetings with his lawyers tonight: the night before that all-important day? If he arrived home late and then left early in the morning, she might miss him entirely, and then it would be too late. And if he lost Becky because of her, she'd never forgive herself. And he might never forgive her. Panic built again.

She'd call his office too. Jessica looked up the number and dialed. His secretary informed her that he was in a meeting. Again, she left a message, asking him to call. She returned to pacing the living room.

A few moments later, she jumped as the shrill ring of the telephone cut the silence of the room. Her immediate reaction was a kind of panic-induced paralysis, and she felt unable to move. Her heart raced as she stood and watched it ring one more time.

Then she leapt for it.

"Jessica?" It was David.

"Yes." Her heart continued to beat so hard that her whole body trembled with the effect.

"I understand you've been trying to reach me." *He had called right back.* Her hopes rose.

"Yes, David. I wonder if I could talk to you. Before tomorrow."

He didn't answer immediately, and she felt a tightness in her chest. *He didn't have time for her. Or maybe his feelings for her had already changed.*

"I'll be home in a couple of hours. Will that be soon enough?"

"Yes." She felt weak with relief. "Yes, that will be fine."

"I'll call you when I get there."

She nodded and then realized that he couldn't see her. "All right." Her voice came out barely a whisper.

"Are you all right, Jessica?"

"Yes! Yes, I'll wait for your call."

She replaced the receiver with trembling hands.

The next two hours passed slowly. She agonized over what she would say to him. In her imagination, he responded positively one moment and negatively the next.

As the two hour interval drew to a close, she went to her bedroom and changed from her cleaning clothes to a fresh pair of white slacks and a blouse. She touched up her make-up and combed her hair. She had returned to the kitchen when, through the window, she saw his car pass by and turn into his driveway. A few minutes later the telephone rang.

"I'm home, Jessica."

He answered the door not knowing what to expect. Not letting himself hope for too much. When he looked down at her, he searched her eyes for a clue of her intent. She looked tired and a little scared, but otherwise he could read nothing.

"Hello, Jessica."

"Hello, David. Thank you for seeing me."

He led her down the hallway to his office. The children's voices carried from the back of the house, but he'd warned them to stay away.

He opened the door of his office, followed her in, and closed the door behind them. He offered her a seat, and then sat on the edge of his desk facing her.

She had been nervous on the way over, but now, in his presence, she felt strangely calm. His hands gripped the edge of his desk, and as she gazed at them, she remembered the tenderness with which they had embraced her the last time she was here. She ached to have them reach for her again. Would they ever do so?

"I've . . . been thinking, David," she began. "I was wrong in dismissing your explanation of why you didn't get back to me the night Cassandra first called you about Becky. And in refusing to understand how emotionally caught up you might be with the fear of losing her." She watched his face, but it remained impassive.

"And it was unfair to accuse you of proposing to me to keep from losing Becky," she continued. "I've never known you to lie or be dishonest about anything before. I pushed you away when you needed me the most." She bit her bottom lip. "I'm asking you to forgive me, David."

His eyes softened. He paused for just a moment, and then he smiled. "I forgive you, Jessica."

Her eyes widened. "You do?"

He nodded. "If you'll forgive me for being a self-righteous, jerk—for presuming that because you didn't conform to my idea of earth mother, you couldn't possibly be right for us."

She looked up into his tired but smiling eyes, and she smiled too. "I forgive you, David."

He pushed himself to his feet and reached for her hands. Pulling her to her feet, he gathered her into his arms. "I've missed you, sweetheart."

Being in his arms again was like a hunger assuaged; it was warmth after a time of freezing cold. She wanted to stay there forever. Then his lips found hers, and her head swam. Their kiss was long and deep.

When next he broke their kiss, he drew back only enough to speak. "Is there anything else you came to tell me, Jessie?"

She could feel his warm breath on her face and basked in his warm gaze. "That we'd better start planning a wedding soon if we want to keep Becky."

His gaze searched hers with sober intensity. "Are you sure, Jessica?"

She placed another soft kiss on his lips and snuggled into his arms. "Very sure."

His arms tightened around her again, this time so firmly that she could hardly breath. He buried his face in her hair. "I felt so empty without you," he whispered hoarsely. Then he pulled back just enough to look into her eyes.

"I love you, Jessica."

Tears filled her eyes, and their lips had barely touched again when they heard the door bell ring. David tensed and listened.

They heard voices in the outer hall and then a knock sounded at his office door. Keeping one arm firmly around Jessica's shoulders he moved to answer it.

Cassandra stood in the hall. She wore jeans and a casual shirt and looked pale and tired. It seemed nobody was sleeping these days.

"I need to talk to you, David."

His arm dropped to Jessica's waist and tightened possessively. "I'm sorry, but you'll have to wait. Jessica and I haven't finished."

"I think you'll want to hear what I have to say."

His jaw tightened and his eyes blazed. "I said we haven't . . ."

Jessica moved in his arms and placed a hand placatingly on his chest. "Maybe you'd better find out what Cassandra has to say, David. I'll wait in the living room." She looked into his troubled eyes and smiled softly. "I'll be here when you've finished."

His hands grasped her upper arms, and his gaze equaled his touch in possessiveness. "Promise me you won't leave." It was both a question and a command.

Now that she was here, he was afraid to let her out of his sight. They'd come together again for such a short time and now were being ripped apart once more. He didn't think he could stand being without her again for even one more day. Whatever happened in this whole mess, he needed her by his side.

When she nodded and reassured him she'd wait, letting go of her seemed the hardest thing he'd ever done. He felt something akin to panic as he watched her go out the door, even as her eyes smiled into his.

All warmth seemed to leave the room with her, and he felt the cold and the hardness rise within him as he faced Cassandra.

"What the devil do you want now, Cassandra? Say what you've come to say. Fast."

But when his eyes finally came to rest on her, and he saw her clearly for the first time since she'd entered the room, her appearance startled him. She looked tired and pale, her eyes swollen and bloodshot. She even seemed thinner. Her expression lacked the cold arrogance of the past and appeared sad now, almost humble. His anger dissipated.

What is it, Cassandra? What's happened?"

She moved to a chair and lowered herself into it. "I can't do it, David," she told him in a thin, strained voice.

He looked at her, puzzled. "You can't do what?"

"I can't take her away from you."

He watched her warily. He didn't trust her. She'd turned on him too many times. "Are you talking about Becky?"

She nodded, and her eyes filled with tears. Her voice dropped to a near whisper. "She's happy here, David. I don't know if I could make her happy. I'd have to be away from her so much." She got up and walked to the window, gazing toward the house next door. "Jessica will nurture her far better than I ever could."

David couldn't believe his ears. What was Cassandra up to? He still didn't trust her and watched her wordlessly.

She seemed to fight to control her emotions as she continued. "I've gotten to know Becky in the time we've spent together recently." She turned back to David. "She's a delightful child. You've done a wonderful job with her, David." She looked back out the window and her voice dropped almost to a whisper. "She belongs here . . . with you."

He took a few steps closer to her, wanting to study the expression on her face, still not convinced she was sincere and still not sure what she was telling him.

"Are you saying you're willing to give up this custody battle for Becky?" he asked cautiously.

She nodded, looking openly into his face. "Yes."

Relief threatened to wash over him, but he restrained it, still wary. He wasn't convinced. "Because you think she'll be better off with me." It was both a statement and a question.

"Yes." She repeated in a whisper, seeming to choke back tears.

But then she brightened a bit as though trying to cheer herself. "But I'll want to take her . . . all the children for visits—for some holidays, and for a month during the summer." She looked up at him hopefully. When he nodded his assent, her aspect brightened a bit more.

She began to move around the room, rubbing her crossed arms briskly. "I do love Derek, David. And the kind of life I have with him is what I want." Her voice took on a note of enthusiasm. "I've enjoyed the study of law, and I think I'll enjoy practicing it. It's exciting and stimulating." She looked up at him as if for approval.

"We all want something different from life, Cassandra. Maybe at last we've all found it." He was beginning to believe this could happen.

"I'm flying back to Boston tomorrow morning, but I'll be in touch."

He nodded.

Her aspect grew somber again. "I'm sorry for all the trouble I've caused you, David . . . both recently and in the past several years. You're a good man. I guess we just want different things."

Her face grew troubled. "You don't think they'll forget me, do you, David?"

He couldn't help reaching out and squeezing her arm. "Of course not, Cassandra. You're their mother, and they do love you. And maybe now that you and I aren't at each others throats any longer, they'll feel free to love you even more." He tried to smile reassuringly. "They can come to see you whenever you like."

A spark of enthusiasm animated her tired features. "When they do come, we'll have wonderful, exciting times!"

Then sobering again, she asked, "Will you marry Jessica?"

David nodded. "Yes."

"I think I knew that almost from the first time I met her. You were different with her somehow. Attentive and protective." She studied him for a moment. "You love her very much, don't you?"

He looked at her somberly and nodded again. "Yes, very much."

She breathed deeply and extended her hand to him. "I wish you every happiness, David."

He took her hand, but then reached to give her a hug. "I think you're doing the right thing, Cassandra. And I, too, wish you every happiness."

She smiled, finally seeming at peace. "Thank you, David. Maybe we can even be friends now."

"I hope so." And then acknowledging the matter was settled, he asked "When did you say you're leaving for Boston?"

"Tomorrow morning. We're invited to a cocktail party in the evening that I don't want to miss. I'll be meeting some of Derek's new colleagues." The thought brought an excited flush to her cheeks.

He smiled, happy for her enthusiasm at the thought of her new life.

"Shall we tell the children?"

He saw a flash of apprehension in her eyes, but in the next moment, she had composed herself again. She nodded and forced a smile.

* * *

After leaving David's office, Jessica sat gingerly on the living room sofa. She felt nervous and ill-at-ease, however, and soon rose again to walk about the room. She examined the pictures on the walls and then walked to the window, looking out on the flower bed just outside: red geraniums, blue violas, and white sweet alyssum. The effect was quite lovely, she thought absently.

Then she heard the low hum of voices from the kitchen and walked toward them.

When she opened the door, four pairs of eyes snapped to look at her. They watched her in silence for several seconds, then Rachael spoke first. "Are you done talking to Daddy?"

"Not exactly. Your mother is in there with him now." Her gaze took in all of them, noting their worried expressions. No one smiled.

Her gaze settled on Becky. It had been over a month since she'd last seen her, and she seemed different: somehow more somber and mature. The little girl acknowledged Jessica's presence, but then continued coloring in her book, unsmiling.

Agatha asked about Jessica's father and then offered her tea. As she accepted, Jessica noticed that Agatha's eyes looked red and puffy.

She asked the children a few questions about their summer activities and received monosyllabic answers. Jessica had finally gotten Tad to talk a little about the upcoming year at school when they heard voices in the living room. Their eyes met one another's worriedly.

The next moment, David pushed the kitchen door open. "Would you all come into the living room, please? Your mother and I would like to talk to you."

Becky climbed down from her chair and marched, like a little soldier, into the next room. They all followed. As Jessica passed David, who continued to hold the door for them all, she whispered an offer to wait for him at home. He grasped the hand that she had laid on his arm, and told her that he would like her to stay.

Still holding her hand, he led her to one of the overstuffed chairs and sat on the arm beside her.

He nodded at Cassandra to begin. Jessica noticed that they looked at each other amicably. A tightness gripped her chest and a tremble shook her body. David must have felt it because he squeezed her hand and winked at her, smiling into her eyes.

Cassandra began. She explained that she planned to marry Derek and would move to Boston immediately. When the children greeted this pronouncement with only worried expressions, she hurried on. She explained that she and their father had decided that all three children would be better off staying in California with him.

Looks of cautious relief now appeared in the eyes of all three children but their expressions still reflected wariness as they glanced at their father and waited for their mother to continue.

Her voice took on a lighter tone as she described the frequent visits they would make to her in Boston. She would take them to see all the wonderful historic places: the campuses of the famous universities—Rachael would have to start thinking about colleges in a few years—the Freedom Trail in Boston, the historic battle sites of Lexington and Concord. They would ride the train to many of these places. It was very different from California, she told them. Sometimes they would come for Christmas, and perhaps it would snow. She would visit them often too—whenever she got a break in her schedule. Cassandra paused and waited hesitantly for their approval.

All three broke into cautious smiles. They began to ask questions about her new apartment. Would there be bedrooms for all of them when they came to visit?

She assured them that she would have plenty of room.

Soon their voices became enthusiastic, and everyone talked at once, smiling and then laughing.

Jessica looked up at David and found him watching her. He squeezed her hand again, and they looked into each other's eyes in wonder at the good fortune that had finally come to them all.

Cassandra asked permission to take the children for an early dinner, before she went back to her hotel to pack for her trip. A few minutes later, David and Jessica stood in the driveway, waving as they all drove off.

When David looked back at her, Jessica couldn't help trying to read what was in his eyes. She had given herself to him emotionally and been convinced of his devotion in return, but Cassandra's announcement had produced a tiny bud of doubt: the fear of loss within her that wouldn't die. Would these new circumstances make any difference between herself and David?

David saw the doubt and knew its cause. He took both of her hands in his own and raised them to his lips. Then he whispered softly. "And now I can ask you to marry me for the sole reason that I'm deeply in love with you and want to spend the rest of my life with you." He saw the doubt disappear, and he saw sheer relief and happiness appear in its stead. A smile spread across her face and lit up her brilliant eyes.

His voice turned husky with emotion as he whispered. "Will you marry me, Jessica Roberts?"

Happiness rose almost to a point of exhilaration. She moved into his arms, and they closed around her. "Oh yes, David, I'll marry you." And then realizing she'd never spoken the words that told of her feelings, she whispered them now. "I love you. So very much."

They held each other, happiness and gratitude and wonder surging through them. Then his lips found hers again, and she melted gratefully into him.

"Whe-e-e-t whe-e-o." They heard the whistle through the mist of their happiness. Looking towards the street, they saw Brad's car, halted at the driveway entrance.

"Can I tell Pat?" he shouted to them.

"Tell the world," David called back.

Epilogue

The morning sun streamed in at the kitchen window. The children's voices chattered excitedly on this, the first day of the new school year. They had been home for almost a month now from a two-week visit with Cassandra in Boston. They didn't go quite as often as originally planned because Cassandra's work kept her busy. This had been their second visit this year, however, and all seemed content with the arrangements.

Jessie and David had married almost a year ago, the wedding having taken place in late September, although the honeymoon had to wait until after Jessica's graduation in December. She didn't write much these days but intended to someday. When life became calmer, she told herself, smiling, as the cry of an infant interrupted her thoughts.

All three children jumped up and ran to the side of the bassinet which stood alongside the kitchen table. They reached for the tiny little hands and spoke gently to the crying baby. Jessica nodded to Rachael's questioning look, and Rachael lifted the three-week-old little boy into her arms. She held him more easily now, Jessie thought as she watched the children happily. She and Agatha exchanged approving glances.

It had been an event-filled year. Sadly, David's mother had passed away in March, but they consoled themselves that she was now past suffering and at rest. David's father had always denied that the care of his wife was a burden, but now that he was more rested and grief had subsided, he seemed to gain a new enthusiasm for life. He visited often and had developed a warm friendship with Jessica's parents.

Jessica's mother and father were also regular visitors to their home. They were thrilled with their new grandchildren and spent frequent weekends in Woodsborough, getting to know them. They stayed in Jessica's house when they came, which she and David had decided to keep as a guest house, a solution which also solved the problem of Jessica's reluctance to part with the old place.

Jessica's father had recovered from his heart attack and had taken the doctor's advice and cut his working hours in half. All the grandparents were due to arrive in a few days for the baby's christening. And since this new child seemed a symbol of the uniting of these two loving families, his name included those of all the male members. Pat and Brad would serve as godparents for little David Thaddeus Henry Alexander Bennington.

Taylor
Daring to love again